Angelina Escapes to Mackinac Island

Suzanne Locascio

O hope you
enjoy it!

~ Suzanne Locascio

B. Nelson Press—Swartz Creek, MI
IISBN: 978-1-7370015-0-8
Library of Congress Control Number: 2021907627
Title: *Angelina Escapes to Mackinac Island*
Author: Suzanne Locascio
Digital distribution | 2021
Paperback | 2021

This is a work of fiction. The characters, names, incidents, places, and dialogue are products of the author's imagination, and are not to be construed as real.

Dedication

To My Grandma Joyce,

You have always been my biggest cheerleader.
Thank you for always being my biggest fan.

Chapter 1

"**Y**our Majesty," a white-wigged man rushed through the doors of the queen's room when her armed guards rushed in front of her majesty, Queen Marie Antoinette. "There are masses of angry peasant women from Paris marching for Versailles. My queen, you must leave!"

"Oh my ███, not here! I will not leave without the king!"

"Pardon me, Your Majesty Marie, you should take the children immediately! Your life is at stake!"

King Louis XVI had been out early hunting, and Marie Antoinette had been at her pleasure house, the Petit Trianon, when they had both been notified that there was a march of raging peasant women that at ten o'clock that morning had left Paris to march to the Palace of Versailles.

"Your Majesty Marie, we must meet their demands," the President of the National Assembly continued. His voice quivered, "there are hundreds of groups of women coming. Jean Joseph Mounier,

1

the President of the National Assembly, spent his time in Paris declaring new laws while he gave himself puffed up airs with long speeches. King Louis XVI tried to ignore the Assembly and refused to recognize Monsieur Mounier as much as he could.

"Thank you for your concern," Queen Marie Antoinette said evenly, with an edge of disdain in her tone. She would not be ordered by a man beneath her status. "The king should be back from hunting soon. When the king arrives, we will discuss our options. Thank you." She nodded again and dismissed him. Then she called for Princess Marie's new governess, Madame de Tourzel. Louis Charles, the Dauphin's daily outing in his little carriage was canceled for the day.

The clock chimed two times. Angelina Savoy was best friend and under-governess to Princess Marie The're'se, oldest child of King Louis XVI and Queen Marie Antoinette, whom the court addressed as Madame Royal. The truth was that the princess was known as a disappointment to the nation because she was not a boy. Princess Marie and Angelina watched the scene from the couch as they had been reading their books. Angelina stared at the queen, scratched her itchy head over her mobcap, and looked over at the princess. Angelina couldn't tell what she was thinking. A bunch of women did not sound very alarming, she thought, we could serve them wine and bread. On the other hand, was there enough bread for everyone to be satisfied? Could there really be hundreds of women coming? Could they really be walking in such steady rain?

Angelina had been educated in the Palace of Versailles with the princess because it helped Madame Royale with her studies, so she would grow to be beautiful and smart. Once Angelina became of age, she would be a lady-in-waiting to the princess. They treated each other as sisters. Angelina was looked at as an older sister because she was thirteen, and Princess Marie was ten. Both had blond hair, but one fairer than the other. Princess Marie had wispy hair the color of honey. Angelina had thick, full hair the color of honeysuckle. Angelina's eyes were hazel. The princess had eyes the color brown. Madame Royale's dark eyes and blond hair made her a striking beauty compared to Angelina. Still, they dressed alike in fine silks, slippers, and ribbons in their hair.

Angelina often pondered what her life would have been like if Queen Marie Antoinette had not taken her in when her mother, one of the queen's ladies-in-waiting, died giving birth to her. Her father, a French soldier, had been killed in America, fighting alongside the Americans in their fight for independence against England.

Angelina watched her queen mother as she spoke to the maids that surrounded her. She ordered them to help with sorting, to help organize the children's clothes, and to pack them into trunks. Angelina was scared to death at the thought of the masses of angry market-women getting closer. This day, she thought, was turning out to be a living nightmare. Frightened, Princess Marie and Angelina put away their diaries and books. Would they leave once the king returned? Where would they go? Would she be able to go with them? What would she pack? She quickly remembered that she had to find her special letter.

When at last, King Louis XVI arrived from the hunt at three o'clock, he rushed upstairs to the queen's quarters to decide what to do. The king never really made decisions on his own. Angelina thought he should be a stronger man without the help of the ministers, or his queen.

Angelina couldn't imagine how hour after hour, these armed, angry women were walking through dark, cold, downpours of autumn rain and dense fog to speak to their king for bread because they and their families were starving.

"Angelina," Queen Marie ordered, "go with Marie to her rooms through the secret passageway. You both need to pack bags to carry inside the carriage, if we have to leave."

"Yes, Madame, Mother." They curtsied and left.

Angelina and Princess Marie carried their belongings in one hand, while walking hand in hand with the other. They were both deep in their own thoughts. Angelina feared for her own life. She needed to find her special letter to put back inside her diary to pack. What would happen to her if the dilemma at the palace went from bad to worse for the royal family?

Currently, the citizens of France were outraged with the royal family. The spring had a few uprisings and riots from the peasants. The worst thing that had happened over the summer was that the Bastille was broken into, the guards were attacked, and the peasants had stolen ammunition and powder.

Since that riot, the citizens became mischievous. They printed pamphlets of Queen Marie Antoinette, with wicked drawings and words. Angelina had not thought anything bad would come because of the pamphlets, but the pamphlets had increased the dislike that the commoners had against the queen, looking for someone to blame. Along with this, France's governing parties were in conflict with each other. She didn't understand how the government worked because it was confusing to her. I will ask Chef Francois, she thought, why everyone is so ready to fight. Everything is in chaos, but I will not starve. When I get hungry later, I can't forget to talk to Chef. He will help me understand what is going on.

They walked into Madame Royale's bedchamber room to see maids already pulling out dresses, sorting what to pack. Angelina suddenly remembered that she had to find the letter now before she forgot, and left the princess to finish sorting out her belongings.

Angelina decided to cheer herself up for a quiet moment by reading her special letter next to the window for light. The letter, which was sent to her by her only living relative, her father's younger brother, Uncle Claude Savoy.

Claude Savoy lived across the Atlantic Ocean on Mackinac Island, in the Northwest Territory of America. He wrote to her that he worked as a fur trapper. How adventurous, she thought, it must be to live in such a faraway place! She didn't know precisely where it was on a map.

Claude Savoy had already left for America before she was born, yet he wrote to her regularly. Writing to her probably out of sympathy, she thought, because she had no parents and they were each other's only family. Claude Savoy wrote to Angelina twice a year since he knew Angelina lived in Versailles. He had learned of Angelina's mother's death from Antoine Savoy, Angelina's father, who informed Claude of her death. Her father had written to Claude to tell him that he had received a note from Versailles stating that his young wife had died in childbirth, and that Angelina's mother had given her over to Queen Marie Antoinette when Angelina's mother was dying. Shortly after, Claude Savoy had been notified that his brother had died in battle.

His latest letter was dated in July of the year 1789. It had taken three months at the start of a new month in October for her to receive it. He wrote that he had married an Ottawa Indian. She reflected that his life got more exciting every time he wrote to her. I wonder if he would like to know me in person. I wonder if he is too self-centered in his own life to want another mouth to feed. Would he want me to live on my own as he did? I wonder if he ever really wonders about me, or if it saddens him to think of me? Does he look like my father?

Angelina stopped the questions in her mind and quickly stood at attention because Queen Marie walked into the room at that moment with a few maids following her. She watched the queen as she spoke softly in a solemn tone to her daughter. Angelina tried to eavesdrop while searching through her closet, and found her tapestry bag. Placing her uncle's letter inside her diary, she put the diary in her bag. She was just about to pack her stays and such when her queen mother summoned her.

"Come here Angelina." Queen Marie called to her, "Do not be afraid. The palace guards will protect us. These women coming to Versailles only want to speak to the king about giving them bread. I am sure they will leave after he speaks to them. Finish what you are doing first, then come to my antechambers through the secret passage. Girls, the king will make everything right again. Do not worry about packing everything because we may not have to leave at all." She and her ladies left.

Angelina was still worried. Princess Marie didn't appear to be afraid. Shouldn't she be more scared than anyone? How could the princess not be scared when the women of France were threatening her family? Maybe she doesn't realize how her life could change by the citizens of France who seemed to hate the royal family.

"Now that everyone is gone," Madame Royale said scheming, "let's hide in the secret passage to hear what my parents are saying. I know they are in my father's bedchamber." The girls slowly opened a small secret door in the wall making sure to shut it before anything looked out of place.

Lots of heated discussions took place as to whether, or not the royal family should ready themselves for the angry market women who wanted to break inside the palace walls. Angelina reached her hand out to hold hands with her dearest friend, who put her hand in Angelina's.

They exchanged nervous smiles and tried to tell each other that it would be over shortly. They listened to endless time-consuming chatter. Should the royal family leave Versailles and go to Rambouillet? It was twice the distance of Versailles from Paris and more secure for the royal family from invasion that awaited them. Was it too late now for the king to decide?

"We must go," Queen Marie begged her husband. "We must go now for the children's safety."

"A runaway king? How could you ask this of me? No man would ever leave his country! We would be welcomed nowhere with no place to live. We will surely die!"

"We can run to Austria," the queen insisted. "We can run to my country! Where my family is!"

Angelina's head was spinning. The blackness and tight space made her nauseous. She broke into a cold sweat, and felt like she needed to vomit. Her world was turned upside down. Now, Angelina's false sense of security was shattered like broken glass. Should she stay with the royal family?

Suddenly, the princess grabbed Angelina's arm, and pulled Angelina into the room with her. She struggled walking into the King Louis's public bedchamber room, which faced the Marble Courtyard. Angelina was petrified that they were going to be in trouble for eavesdropping and coming into the room uninvited. The girls curtsied deeply while Angelina tried not to vomit or faint. The king stood to acknowledge them.

"What is it?"

"May we stay with you?" Madame Royal asked.

The king nodded. "Yes."

The girls sat on the couch. Angelina was quiet, relieved to be able to sit down to compose herself. There was no answer to what to do. The wild women could be there at any moment. What would happen when the women arrived? Would they be civil, or act like a pack of wild animals?

Suddenly, they began to hear an echoing, distant uproar like thunder. Angelina got up and looked out the window. She slowly moved the curtain aside alongside with the other ladies-in-waiting who served the queen. Angelina stared out the window at the hundreds, turned into what looked like thousands of women. More and more merchant's wives, the butchers' wives, the fishermen's wives, the baker's wives, and the lower-class street women walked up into the outer courtyard to demand bread and grain from their king.

"We want bread! We want bread!" the crowd shouted over and over as they marched up Grand Avenue de Paris. Angelina watched as the women passed through the main gate, with its golden coat of arms representing the Horn of Plenty and the Crown. Angelina gasped in shock.

"Only royal blood passes though those gates," Angelina muttered under her breath, "Even the aristocracy is forbidden."

Madame Auguie, the queen's head lady in waiting, turned around, and looked to the king. "Your majesty, they have broken down the gate and are coming into the Marble Courtyard."

Angelina observed the first set of angry starving women as they approached Monsieur Jean Mounier. Madame Royale finally looked out the window to see what was happening. The girls stood stunned looking down at the mob of peasant women. Angelina stared at the Parisian women trying to see their faces and hair that had fallen out of their mobcaps. Unexpectedly, she saw men. Angelina studied them over to see if she recognized any aristocracy, courtiers, or any other familiar faces as they screamed, hollered, and waved weapons such as guns, pikes and staves in the air ready to vandalize Versailles. Would she have to suffer the same fate as the royal family, if the royal family was captured and taken away from Versailles? Where would the government of France imprison the royal family? Would the angry citizens send them to the Bastille to torture them because the citizens felt their king and queen had abandoned them? Shouldn't I leave here to go to America to find my uncle? She had a feeling this was to be her only plan to survive the fate of Versailles. Undecided and self-doubting, Angelina couldn't help think that her plan was unrealistic at the same time. She could never leave, she thought, she was only a child.

"Girls! Get away from the windows," King Louis XVI scolded them.

The girls left and sat back on the couch. There was no going now. They couldn't escape even if they tried. There was no escaping the citizens that had come to see their sovereign. Louis Charles cried in his nurse's lap, so the king settled him onto his lap. Princess Marie's eyes looked like to Angelina wide open and worried. Angelina prayed a silent prayer for wisdom and strength. Everyone looked to King Louis XVI to hear something positive from him. Still, the king held to his decision to stay at Versailles.

There were hundreds of market-women still arriving as late in the day as five and six o'clock. The royal guards stood at attention near the locked doors. The clock chimed six times, when a guard knocked, and the door was opened for him to enter at the king's command. The kings guard, a Black Guardsman marched in with a written message. It was from the Marquis, to now with a new title, General Lafayette. It confirmed that he was bringing the National Guardsmen to help secure the situation.

"My king, the message was delivered from one of Lafayette's men. It states he and 15,000 armed guardsmen and 7,000 latecomers are headed for Versailles. That is all the message says. The citizens now demand that a delegation of peasant women be allowed to speak to you."

Angelina looked up to King Louis XVI. She saw a relieved look in his expression. The message encouraged the royal family to think that they had the time to sit back and relax with the belief that everything would be back to normal, and no one would be killed nor, would they have to leave Versailles.

What if it was a false hope to trust your faith in someone else when there are so many people outside wanting and waiting to kill the royal family? What if the king and queen are fooling themselves out of fear? The king should be thinking of us, Angelina thought, he is such a coward! The royal family should have left for Rambouillet already. They wouldn't be in fear of their lives and neither would she. If I were the queen, I would have left without the king.

King Louis XVI turned to his queen, "Good to know General Lafayette is finally on his way. All will be well. You shall see my queen that we have nothing to fear. I have to meet with my ministers in the Oeil-de-Boeuf antechamber. We may have a peaceful night after all. I will come back later with how we will act according to their wishes. I am sure everything will be settled by the time I come back to you and the children."

Queen Marie nodded in agreement, and King Louis XVI left.

"We want bread!" The mob still chanted as the masses of citizens raised their voices together for their cause. "We want bread!"

They hollered to be heard by their king and queen. Angelina wanted to see what was happening outside. Slowly, she got up from the couch since King Louis XVI had left. She walked to the windows to stare down at the riotous crowd armed and ready to fight. Angelina felt deeply sorry for their misery. She wanted to walk out on the balcony to get a closer look at the soaking wet, filthy women's dresses, and see how ragged they were. She noticed that the masses of people had grown twice the size now. She would be terrified if the women saw her, Angelina thought. They would think of her as a royal. Fearing for her life got her thinking. She had to start making a plan and be prepared for the worst.

She felt sorry for how poor these women looked. Wet hair stuck to their faces showing underneath their hoods and mobcaps. All these women were so thin with sunken-in cheeks, exposing their teeth, and some had no teeth at all. All of them, she thought, looked like they were near starved to death!

Within the hour, a small group of market-women had been invited into Versailles to speak to their king. King Louis XVI was weighing over his options with his ministers in his receiving room when the small group of women leaders, who represented the masses of market-women were escorted by his majesty's guards outside of the Salon L'Oeil-de-Boeuf antechamber door.

King Louis XVI eventually agreed to meet with one woman in his antechamber in his apartments, "whose appearance and dress was neither misery nor an abject condition."

Madame Royale and Angelina grew bored waiting for something to do. The princess giggled, and elbowed Angelina's arm, "Let's go through the secret passageways and get a good look at the courtyard."

"Yes," Angelina whispered, "but let's say we are going to get some food."

"Mother, we are going the secret way to the kitchen for a snack."

"I don't think it is a good idea."

"Mother," she whined, "Angelina is going with me. I won't be on my own."

The girls waited for permission to leave. They watched Queen Marie as she rose from her chair, walked towards Angelina, bent down and kissed her on the forehead, and then kissed her daughter's forehead.

"You two be careful going down to the kitchen for your snack. We are to dine for dinner soon," She turned to face Angelina, "you can go down to the kitchen when we dine, and make a plate for yourself."

"Yes, Madame Mother," they said at the same time, curtsied and left.

Once the girls reached a window that looked down to the courtyard, both girls were astonished by the near-nakedness of the market women.

"I have never seen such poverty before," remarked Princess Marie, humbled. "I thought I saw a few men down there."

"Yes, I did too. Some dressed up in disguise as women."

Angelina was intrigued as well, but kept her thoughts to herself. As she looked down at the mob, Angelina felt she should be with these market-women since she was not a pureblood member of the royal family. However, she felt blessed by God that she was well taken care of by them. She didn't know what to say due to her conflicted opinions.

The girls circled back to the king's public bedchamber. They didn't want to miss a thing. King Louis XVI was back in his public bedchamber as the clock chimed seven times. Angelina was getting hungry. No doubt that the angry masses were already hungry, and going nowhere for the night.

Angelina looked over at Queen Marie. She had noticed when she had looked at the queen's expression, she thought, something in her face had changed. Angelina couldn't decide whether the queen was mad, sad or scared.

The majority of the crowds remained. Angelina wondered why the groups still lingered, if the king has already pleased his people? The uproar from the courtyard reached louder than ever up to the royal family. Monsieur Jean Mounier who was standing next to Louis XVI left to investigate.

After what seemed like an hour, the minister returned with a sheet of parchment paper with a shaking hand.

The king read it over, outraged, "These women do not trust the king's word?"

"Please sign it," Queen Marie advised him, "then we will have a peaceful night."

Louis XVI accepted and signed without hesitation, the Declaration of the Rights of Man and the August degrees. Monsieur Jean Mounier left to show the masses that the agreement was signed. The king did not comment on how he felt. Angelina noticed he was deep in thought. His eyes looked toward the floor ashamed to look at the queen, or his children. Angelina walked over to the window to see what was happening, hoping that the king wouldn't notice, and scold her again.

Within a few minutes, the chaos began to disperse. She spied down at the women as they hugged and congratulated each other. Some left, and walked back up Avenue de Paris making their way back to Paris. However, the majority of masses of women and men lingered in the courtyard. She watched as the people used the torches that they had carried to start campfires in the royal court. Without wanting to ask permission, Angelina announced, "Madame Mother, I am going down to the kitchen." She curtsied and left.

Chapter 2

Huge hallways, rooms beyond rooms, the marble floors went as far as the eye could see. Everything gleamed and was as grand as the other side of the palace. Her stomach gurgled. She knew the staircase well that took her down to the basement floor. The odious smells of onions tainted the air. She tracked the stench around the winding corridors, inhaling the mouthwatering aromas of baked baguettes and meats being roasted. Stopping, she stood by the door of an enormous room with stewstoves, hearths and spits.

"Boy!" She shouted at a small boy wearing a dirty apron near the door. "Sausages, for Madame Royale! Quick!" He jumped, startled, and rushed to put sausages in a pewter dish.

"And some bread! Hurry!"

He placed a petite baguette across the sausages and handed it to her. She turned, and left without thanking him. She had learned growing up in Versailles that servants really don't talk to one another, and especially if they know their status was beneath them. The higher servants liked to boss everybody, but no one bossed her around to do this or that. Most everyone knew that her boss was the princess. She liked that her servitude was at least a clean job because she didn't like the idea of being a dirty kitchen girl. Since she bossed the kitchen boy around, he logically felt she had outranked him. She played him to think she was important, so she could get her way.

The meat was delicious. Grease dripped down Angelina's chin onto the plate. She wiped the dish clean with the bread. She carried her plate back to the basement kitchen. After, she looked around to find the Head Chef, Chef Francois, who was the closest man to her as a father.

"What did you think?" Chef Francois asked her indelicately. "That you were one of the children of France?" She had found him outside by the kitchen door, getting some fresh air drinking a glass of red wine. She had confessed to him regarding her uncle, Claude Savoy. She also confessed her feelings of staying with the princess. She confessed how twisted her feelings were over how she felt disloyal to her best friend, and how she was at a war with herself over what to do.

"I don't want to feel like a traitor!" Angelina covered her mouth in shock when she yelled at him. "I don't want to be trapped with them and end up in a prison with the royal family, but am I expected to go because I serve the king's daughter?"

"You are not the princess," replied Chef. "Be happy that you are not because they are in serious trouble! You have a way out!"

"I don't see it that way! I have no one!"

"Mademoiselle," as he tried to comfort her, "you said you have an uncle in the New World. I am sure that you have been given pay for your services to that spoiled princess. Do not be naïve and follow in their footsteps. Take those savings and run to America! You don't understand how the world works since you have been spoiled living in Versailles all your life. You have a fair chance to work in a shop to be an apprentice. You need money to buy an apprenticeship. I am old and stuck here, but you have a chance to live a good life that is yours."

"The princess used to say to me that I would be her head lady in waiting. She promised to always take care of me."

"You can't go with them," he frowned at her, closed his eyes and rubbed his eyebrows with his hands. "It is unacceptable," he opened his eyes, and stared straight into hers. "You are stronger than you think. You have to believe that you can survive because we are all leaving! The people of France are here to stay until they take the royal family back to Paris as their prisoner. You are going to have to

21

learn how to survive on your own. I'm not trying to be mean." He grabbed and hugged her hard. "I love you. I want you to go to America, dear girl."

"But it's not the princess's or the queen's fault?"

"I know that, but the people blame her. You have seen the pamphlets of her with the dirty pictures. They accuse her of all France's money troubles. They blame her for the increased taxes that they believe pay for her lavish clothes, her lace made new every day, her extravagant buying of jewels and shoes. They blame her for the extreme waste of flour with her pastries. I know because I am the one who creates them!"

"Everybody loves Versailles' pastries! She dresses plain unless she is to make an appearance to the citizens of France. She does not spend money on jewels because they are gifted to her."

Chef hesitated for a moment, then resumed his work while he continued to talk. "Maybe you should think about stealing the queen's jewels before the women end up taking them. You mark my words. These women are angry, greedy, and have nothing to lose by taking something of value to feed themselves. They are not just here for bread and wine."

"I don't know if I could ever steal from our queen."

"You may not have a choice." Chef Francois stopped his work, wiped his hands on a towel, and hugged her again, whispering in her ear so no one would hear him. "If you get the chance, girl. You take it! The biggest jewels you can carry because that will be your money to America."

"Ok." She hugged him with eyes full of tears of sorrow for everything that was happening in her world…. Leaving him, leaving the princess that was her best friend, leaving Versailles, and leaving France for an entirely new life. She feared she was not ready for it. "Chef, please tell me about the government now? I remember you saying something a long time ago about the nobles, clergy, and the commoners?"

"Oui," he started, "Yes! I know you hear stories from the royal family, so here is the truth of what has happened since the spring. In May, do you remember when the town was overrun because of all wealthy aristocracy, the nobles, courtiers, and other rich men that had come to Versailles for the meeting of the Estates General?"

"Only a little really," she looked ashamed at the floor because she felt deep down that she should know more about her country, especially about how the royals and other men represent France. She needed to listen patiently to learn, she thought, about her country and all its troubles and why.

"France has three different classes of people that they name differently in the Estates General that once was. Chef Francois simplified the meeting of representatives, or delegates that they called themselves from the three states of France-the nobility, the clergy, and the commoners. Each state got one vote as a whole. You understand, one vote for the nobles, one vote for the clergy, and one vote for the commoners. The nobles and the clergy always agree."

"Doesn't it hurt to overrule the majority of the people? The noble and the clergy don't go hungry. Our winters have been so hard from what you have told me yourself. You said the crops of wheat grew poorly this last year. Is this why the commoners are here?"

"Yes, Mademoiselle," Chef continued. "We need to open all our food stores, or Versailles will be ripped apart. We are lucky we work in the court of Versailles. The country is falling apart, and the royal family could do something. Instead, they act like they don't notice how their people blame them for their struggles".

"The queen is not to blame. She came from Austria. Can we please stop talking about her? I am soon to be a woman. Just because I am a woman, am I to blame for our country's problems?"

"Everyone already thinks that she rules the king. I know how she likes the excess of using the king's money for her own pleasures like for building her own chateau, the Petit Trianon. Our country is in the arms of an Austricheinne. She has ruined

Versailles, and she will destroy you, if you stay with her."

"That's not true! She would never hurt me!" Angelina rushed out of the kitchen past him, through the winding corridor, and up the staircase as bile rose in her throat. She turned and ran to find the nearest corner to puke in. No one saw, or heard her. If someone would have, they would have come to see who it was out of curiosity to see. Straightening her mobcap, she looked down at her dress to see if she got any vomit on it. Fortunately, she saw that none got on it. She went back to talk to Chef, and acted like she never had a temper tantrum.

"I understand you perfectly that you think I need to leave Versailles," she returned to Chef. "I am sorry about my bad behavior. Please tell me more about the government with the representatives."

Chef explained that the Estates General was the special meeting of delegates from the three states of France - the nobility, the clergy, and the commoners.

"For days nothing. The king was silent for hours listening to negotiations. Everything the Third Estate tries to accomplish gets voted down by the noble and the clergy, who won't give an inch of their equality." He exhaled in frustration. He was still ranting about the unfairness of it all.

"The nobles and the clergy refuse to pay taxes. They don't want to change. Why would they want to change? The Third Estate pays for all their luxuries, in my opinion."

"Yes, I remember now," she interrupted. "And then the Third Estate walked out. They met separately at another place, calling themselves the National Assembly. The Third Estate said that a new government should not be ruled by a king that they felt did not care for the ordinary citizens even though they were starving. The new representatives act upon what the commoners want. All the commoners want is bread and grain from the royal storehouses."

She started to question her loyalty to the royal family. If a king was unfair, she thought, was it wrong to turn against him? The Americans had turned against the British king and won their independence. It was now going to be the same here, she thought, the king's and queen's glory days are over.

"I know what you are saying, and I hear you. I do want to go to America. I have to think about what I need to say to the princess."

"Do what you have to do!" He looked her straight in the eyes. "This is your life! Not hers!" She was touched by how he was trying to convince her to fight for her life. She hugged him again, "I will see you soon to tell you what my plans are." She walked out, hiding the tears in her eyes.

Angelina went back to her bedchamber to pack her belongings in her tapestry bag. The servant to Madame Royale's bedchamber had been waiting for her.

"Madame Royale desires you to dine with her immediately."

"Please tell the princess that I will be humbled to be included to dine with her and the royal family." Angelina walked away with a heavy heart knowing that this was to be the last meal she was to attend with the royal family. It was an order, not an invitation. She washed her face and hands, and prepared her hair with her best mobcap that was trimmed with lace. She put on a soft yellow silk dress. After, she ran with quick steps to the formal dining room.

The princess sat at the far end of the table with Madame Tourzel, their governess, sitting across from her. Princess Marie turned and looked at Angelina. Something was cold in her attitude towards her. She smiled at Princess Marie, hoping that she would smile back, but the princess only looked down at her plate.

"You should have come back earlier," Madame Royale looked up at her, greeting her in a snotty tone. "You have been gone for a long time. What have you been doing? Thinking about running away?"

Angelina blushed. "No, I am your best friend." Embarrassed by the princess in front of the royal family, anger raged up in her. How could Princess Marie, her best friend, humiliate her in public? What could she say?

"I am sorry," was all she could say since she did not want to cause a scene. "I couldn't fix my hair properly, so it took longer."

"Girls," declared King Louis XVI, "the trouble is practically over. My people are leaving, and all will be well again. General Lafayette will soon be here to calm the people's worries and protect Versailles. The troops have returned to their barracks. We will have a peaceful night," he said as he turned to his queen.

Queen Marie nodded.

"The king has heard their demands and agreed to release the wine, grain, beer and bread to them. Now, the women will go back to Paris. Queen Marie looked at the girls, as she tried to comfort them. "Girls, No one intends to harm us."

Chapter 3

Madame Royale retired to her bedroom on the ground floor, Angelina followed. Angelina could not sleep and didn't try. The roaring fire popped. She got up, turned the logs over with the iron fire poker to lower the fire down, ogled at the colors of the fire, and watched the embers fall into the fireplace grate. The clock in the room chimed mid-night, when they heard noises in the hall.

"Go and see what is going on," ordered Madame Royal to the guard who stood by the door.

"It probably was a guard on the midnight post walkarounds," Angelina said.

"It could be a man disguised as a woman trying to break into our bedroom," Princess Marie snapped at her. "Let's go through the secret passage."

"Marie, I have to tell you something. You know that I have the uncle that writes to me from America. I want to go to America to be with him. I love you, but I want to leave France. I need your support so that I can get on a good, safe ship over the Atlantic. Please don't be mad at me!"

"You can't leave us to go to America! You must stay with me! We are not going anywhere! We are not leaving Versailles!"

"Marie, I want to!"

"You can't. I forbid it!" Princess Marie squeezed Angelina's hands so tight that it hurt her. Angelina tried to pull away, but the princess held her. "You are not going anywhere because it is not safe to leave. You would have to walk with those ugly women. What if they try to harm you and rob you?" She sighed, let Angelina's hand go, and dropped her eyes. "Please, don't go. You are my best friend. I don't know what could happen to you. Please stay."

"Yes, tis true," Angelina answered. She realized that she could get assaulted from the angry mob. Princess Marie was right. Those wild women were not just going to let a spoiled child from Versailles pass through their ranks with her belongings intact. If only, she thought, if only my uncle would come for me! Her heart ached for the princess. Angelina saw the love in the princess's eyes that she had for her, but Angelina didn't want to stay with them if they were going to be held as France's prisoners.

"Let's find my father."

They dressed themselves with nightrobes over their nightgowns and put their bedtime mobcaps on. Sneaking out, they opened the secret door hidden in the wall of their bedchamber to enter and exit the secret passageways. The girls tiptoed to the middle of Versailles back into the king's public bedchamber. It was empty because he slept in his private bedchamber in his private apartment. They gazed out from a window at the center of the courtyard. The Marble Court was filled with campfires and tents. The campfires looked like the stars in the night sky as there were too many to count. The girls stared out from the window to watch the citizens still setting up tents, while still more citizens were slowly moving through the cold rain drinking, or trying to stay warm.

"I can't believe they want to sleep in the courtyard," Marie exclaimed. "It's disgusting!"

"There's still more coming," said Angelina stunned. "I see torches, so that means more people."

They strained to see through the blackness. Another group of people were approaching down Grand Avenue de Paris, dimly lit by the torches they held. Mounted guardsmen marched at the front of the incoming citizens, with a man on a white horse in the lead.

"That horse is so beautiful," said Angelina. "A wealthy man rides that horse."

"That is General de Lafayette," exclaimed Princess Marie, sighing in relief that he had finally arrived. "Let's hurry to eavesdrop on my father when he meets with him."

They rushed back into the secret door into the secret passages. Soon enough, the girls laid their fingertips flat against the door and slowly opened it a crack. They waited in secret for the General to be received into the Oeil-de-Boeuf, which was the infamous receiving room, named for its window shaped like a bull's eye. The girls snuck their heads around the door to take a peek at him without being seen by the king, or anyone else who was there in the room. A few moments later, General Lafayette came through the door, they unmistakably saw him. He wore a white wig to make his best appearance to King XVI even overtired as he was, and covered in mud from his boots to the ends of this wig. They snuck back in, keeping the door opened a crack to hear them.

"Your Majesty," his voice full of enthusiasm as he sounded strong even though he had been up for over twelve hours. "I pledge my allegiance to you as the head of the National Guard. The revolutionaries have surrounded the palace. The march of women started because they were encouraged by the rebel revolutionaries. The peasant women robbed the Paris city armory for their weapons to march here at Versailles to encourage you to give them what they want. My men of the National Guard are here to protect you."

"But yet, they have not," the king interrupted.

"I will control the citizens," Lafayette replied, his voice stern, but still his body was fighting against exhaustion. "They will back down, if we give the women bread and grain from Versailles' storehouses. They want you and the government to come to Paris to be established there."

"I have already opened the storehouses. I will not leave Versailles. It is my home. Why would we have to leave?"

"The citizens are not leaving here until you leave with them."

"We will decide in the morning."

Lafayette spoke in whispered voices that the girls couldn't hear. Princess Marie slowly let the door close. They hurried through the passages back to their room, climbed back into their beds, gazed at each other one more time, and tried to sleep away their fears over the coming day.

Angelina felt more awake than ever. She was terrified to have to find the courage to leave her beloved country. How was she to survive and make a life for herself? How could she leave her best friend?

Chapter 4

Gunshots ripped through the air, and shrieks and more screams. The girls woke up spooked, sat up, and the guards in the girls' bedroom stood at attention ready to protect them. Both girls froze with fear in their beds, it was not yet daybreak. Angelina jumped up in her bed again. The jumping up started to annoy her since it was only the clock ringing at the six o'clock hour. I am not going to jump, she thought, at every little noise. They wondered if there was any news of a truce, or if they had missed anything. They changed clothes, put on mobcaps, and with the guards protection ran to her little brother's guardhouse. They stared out of the window that overlooked the Marble Courtyard. A band of soldiers of National Guardsmen who had sided with the angry mob had charged through the inner courtyard. The Black Guard, who were King Louis XVI's soldiers, tried to overtake them without wasting bullets. A hail of bullets from the mob brought down a few of the king's guardsmen. Suddenly, the girls heard footsteps running throughout the hallways. Angelina's body jumped in shock from the sounds of more gunshots, shrieks, shouts, and more gunfire that pierced her ears.

The girls left the window, and sprinted through the secret passages to the door of Queen Marie's bedchamber. The girls heard screams and yells from outside her door. The girls burst in to her room.

"Oh, my ▓▓," shouted Queen Marie alarmed!" You two scared me. I thought you were the women coming to get me!"

The queen half-naked, her favorite lady-in-waiting, Madam Augie, dressing the queen frantically without tying up all her stays and petticoats.

"Girls, pay attention," Queen Marie ordered. Everyone followed Queen Marie through the secret staircase. "We must get to the king's apartments," she shouted. They are trying to break into my room!"

When they reached the door to the king's private bedchamber, they found it was locked. Madam Augie pounded on it, shouting for the king. No guard answered. In a panic, they turned and hurried back in the secret passages. Somewhere they would have to find safety before they were murdered. How could she get away to steal some of the queen's jewels when they were already running for their lives, if they made it out alive. She needed to find protection for herself with money for the journey to America. Angelina needed to find a time to take what was necessary before horrible looters tried to get to the queen's jewels first. She was feeling sick with fear, if she could even be brave enough to steal. The butterflies in her stomach fluttered within her, she knew she had no choice now since the citizens were already trying to kill the royal family.

King Louis XVI panted hard, short of breath, coming towards them with Louis Charles in his arms. King Louis XVI knocked on the door seven times in a musical way, which then a servant opened the secret door to his public bedchamber. Everyone in the royal family met inside safe all together, including the king's sister, Madam Elizabeth, along with Madam Tourzel and the Princess of Lamballe.

The king was rattled. "Where is my brother?"

His sister replied, "He abandoned us last night."

Angelina and Princess Marie sat on the couch. If the king had regretted leaving, he was silent. King Louis XVI nodded. Princess Marie took Angelina's hand. How could the princess show such kindness and take my hand, Angelina thought, when I am supposed to be brave and serve her. Outside the door, loud, thunderous footsteps, and screams were heard. The door flew open. Angelina jumped.

General de Lafayette charged in with his silver blood-spattered sword upwards in his right hand.

"My king, I am here! Are you hurt?"

Outside the door, Angelina eyed a man wearing a blue uniform lying lifeless.

"No! What is the status, General?"

"Sire!" General Lafayette bowed to his king. "As you know since six o'clock this morning, a small group of rioters broke into the palace to get to the queen." He turned and bowed to his queen. "I am sorry my queen." He bowed to Queen Marie again in apology, "that the rioters tried to attack you." He turned back to the king. "The Black Guards have walked throughout the palace to bolt every entrance they could. Some of the guardsmen were caught off guard and fired at, killing a young soldier. His death has caused the mob to storm Versailles. The citizens have outrun the outnumbered National Guardsmen and Black Guard. Two of my guards, Monsieur Miomandre and Monsieur Tardivet were brutally murdered. They have put Tardivet's head on a spike. I have managed to calm down the majority of the National Guardsmen, and we are reconciling with the surviving guards."

King Louis XVI had decided that his appearance was needed in order to make peace with the rioters.

Angelina was appalled by the violence. She could not get her mind off the blood-spattered sword. How many had General Lafayette struck down? Where was Chef Francois? She could hardly gather her wits. Beside her, Princess Marie looked confused as her eyes danced back and forth between her parents. Louis Charles was crying. Angelina wanted to cry with him in her arms. The masses during the night had been tamed with offers to the peasants with trays of food and drink passed around. However, as the sun rose, the cold and hunger drove the drunken revolutionaries, which was what they were calling themselves, to once again try to break into Versailles.

General Lafayette opened the door to the balcony overlooking the Marble Courtyard and stepped out to charm the crowds. Shouts roared up to the balcony in cheering for him. After, General Lafayette came back into the room, he looked at King Louis XVI. "The citizens are ready to greet you," General Lafayette implored to his king. "You will be safe out on the balcony to help stabilize the tension among the crowds."

"Yes, of course," King Louis XVI rose and stepped out to the balcony, closing the door, so Louis Charles would hopefully calm down from crying. Angelina didn't overhear what the king was saying to the crowds. She didn't want to listen. She retreated to the other side of the room. Queen Marie was trying to stop the little Dauphin from crying while she rocked him. Princess Marie rose to sit by her mother and grasped her mother's arm.

"My queen," announced General Lafayette, as the balcony door opened and he walked back in, "your appearance can make peace with the crowds. You must speak to them!"

Thousands of voices of vulgar names and catcalls echoed through the air. Queen Marie rose, and held hands with her daughter. She adjusted the infant boy onto her hip. She strolled onto the balcony, silent and unsmiling, taking them with her. Princess Marie's face was almost green, which was the last thing Angelina saw before she escaped through the secret back door to Queen Marie's bedchamber. Now was her only chance to make it to the queen's jewelry cabinet.

Angelina cautiously moved through the secret passage to the queen's antechamber making sure no one saw her. Once in the room, Angelina eyed the queen's jewelry box. Out of fear and desperation, Angelina ran over to the Schwerdfeger Jewel Case. Without a second thought, she stuffed as many necklaces, earrings, and rings, as she could into her stays and petticoats under her dress.

The queen won't need them now, she thought, if they are to escape with their lives. I will need these to survive on my own. I can show them to the queen later, if I do end up going along with them.

Angelina's ears perked up when she overheard women's voices inside the palace walls, and listened for their footsteps running up the staircase. Quickly, Angelina pushed away the wall tapestry to reveal the secret door. She hid silently in the secret passageway, and crouched down into a ball. Angelina was terrified that she would be found. Her emotions overwhelmed her, she grieved quietly sobbing. Would she ever see her best friend and the rest of the royal family ever again after the mob left? How long would Angelina have to stay hidden in the secret passageway? When could she come out so that she didn't starve to death? Angelina knew she would have to wait until the voices faded away. It was still too early to know if the royal family planned to go to Paris. Eventually, she came out when it was quiet, and fixed her face in the queen's mirror to make appearances getting back to the royal family, hoping that nobody noticed that she had left.

Angelina's eyes were opened wide with the truth that now confronted her. She panicked that she had no place to call home, no blood family who could take her in, and no trade learned to make a living. As she wiped her red, swollen, soaked face, Angelina tried to calm herself to realize that she did have family and the queen's jewels. Angelina had her Uncle Claude Savoy, who lived in America. She was relieved that she had gotten away with stealing, feeling a new kind of courage. Her plan was secure now knowing that she would have the money by pawning off Queen Marie's jewels, so she could pay for the passage on a ship to go to America, to find, and live with her Uncle Claude Savoy.

Angelina treaded carefully back into the room. The entire royal family looked gray, but the king remained calm. Angelina looked around the room. Where was Queen Marie with the Dauphin and Princess Marie?

Angelina trembled with fear from head to toe when she saw the silhouettes of them still on the balcony. While controlling her emotions, she sat back on the couch looking like she never left. She came back, she thought, just in time. The three of them slowly stepped back into the room, and sat together next to Angelina. Madam Royale was trembling when she started sobbing, and the Dauphin was screaming crying.

"No, children!" shouted the masses that echoed into the room. "No children!" Then another multitude of citizens chanted, "To Paris! To Paris!"

"My queen, please, you must go out on the balcony one more time without the children. There are at least fifty thousand strong out there wanting to see you."

From the open balcony doors, Angelina listened to the continuous shouted insults and threats from the masses. Queen Marie Antionette strolled back out to the balcony once more, bowed her head to the masses, her shoulders were trembling from what Angelina could see with her hands holding the balcony railing. Then, Angelina watched as Queen Marie stretched her arms out across the balcony railing while she bowed her head to France's citizens.

"They are so ungrateful!" Princess Marie whispered in anger. "My father gave them everything they asked! What do they want?"

"They are so hungry that they can't help it," Angelina countered, speaking softly. Angelina was frustrated because her best friend was being ignorant to the people's needs from the trauma that they were starving. "They are starved."

The princess looked up to Angelina, shocked. "How can you say that when you know my father signed their agreement for food?" Princess Marie snapped at her, keeping her voice down. "Now, all they are to me are drunken worthless women and men killing Versailles guards. They threaten to kill my father and my mother! Are you taking their side?"

"No," sighed Angelina. "Your family is my family. If your mother had not shown me a great favor in letting me live in great wealth, I don't know where I would be. Of course, I would be starving too. I would probably live in a dingy orphanage, or some poor foster home working as a farm girl, or worse."

"Do you think you would have had the courage to march with these peasants?"

"No," Angelina whispered. "I am not an adult like these women." Angelina scooted beside her being careful not to move the jewels inside her stays, and forced the princess to take her hand. "Marie, look at me. I don't want to leave you. I love you. You are my sister. You are my best friend. If I had never met you, my life would not be as wonderful as it is with you. Please understand, if my parents were alive than I would still be a commoner like those women."

"Yes," she whispered. Princess Marie sighed, hesitating to speak. "I do know that you have been favored. You are my sister, and you have to be with us because we are family. Our lives will be happy again after these peasants leave. Whatever happens, you will not leave me. We must stay strong and stay together. We need each other."

Angelina nodded in agreement to satisfy her, but her plans had been made.

As the girls looked up towards the balcony, the echoes of the chants grew louder to cheers.

"Long live the queen! Long live the king! Long live Lafayette!" General Lafayette had calmed the masses. He had somehow pleased the crowds again to bring peace. Queen Marie sauntered back

43

into the room. King Louis XVI looked gray and weak, but Queen Marie remained reserved.

"Thank you, you have spoken for us," Queen Marie stated to General Lafayette. "Please, how can we save the National Guard and the Black Guard? We need no more deaths at Versailles."

"Sire," General Lafayette, turned and looked to King Louis XVI. "You must go out on the balcony and show that you are wearing the cockade of France's revolutionaries."

King Louis XVI looked like a frightened schoolboy. Angelina watched his face fall from being defeated. If he didn't like being bossed around by General Lafayette, he didn't show it.

"Sire, please come out on to the balcony," begged Lafayette, "I pledge my service to you." He led King Louis XVI out. Both girls watched through the opened balcony doors as General Lafayette removed the king's white cockade off his hat that was part of his royal uniform - the symbol of the king. Everyone watched as the general dropped it over the balcony railing. Next, General Lafayette took off the tricolor cockade that was decorated in colors of blue, white and red from his own hat, pinned it onto the king's hat, and shook hands with him.

Great thunderous applause was heard from the thousands.

"Long live France! Long live France!"

General Lafayette accompanied King Louis XVI back inside.

"Notify all the guards to put on the tricolor cockade," Lafayette ordered to the other guards in the room. Angelina stared at General Lafayette as he bowed to the king,

"My king, you must leave to go to Paris. You must, Sire. It is time."

King Louis XVI looked melancholy as he glanced around the room like in a trance from being worn down with defeat.

"Tell the guards to order the carriages," King Louis XVI requested, "Order all the carriages, General. We leave today."

Chapter 5

The General bowed to his king. General Lafayette left and announced to the masses, reassuring them that he was going to lead the escort of King Louis XVI and the royal family to Paris. In Versailles, servants filled leather trunks with the things the royal family needed. The king's ministers created prioritized lists of formal documents to bring.

"Where are we going?" Queen Marie asked.

"To the Tuileries Palace," answered the king.

I need to pack as many clothes as I can now, Angelina considered, I need to try to stay after the royal family leaves. I want to make sure I say my good-byes to Chef Francois, and look around just in case to make sure I did not forget something. I know there are more jewels. I will collect them, if the Queen Marie hasn't taken them with her, she thought, before vile looters get to them. She will already think that looters robbed her, if she sees some are missing.

"Marie, I am leaving to pack my things," Angelina whispered.

"You must not leave!" Princess Marie whispered, so nobody would hear them. "You could get killed! I am going to tell my mother! She will not let you leave!"

In Angelina's indecision, she did nothing because she didn't want the princess ruining her plans. Angelina was afraid that with Marie threatening her, she would tell on her to her mother. Madame Mother Queen Marie could possibly force her to stay, which she wasn't going to do. Princess Marie took Angelina's silence as meaning she had won in their quarrel. The princess smiled feeling victorious.

"I just need to pack my bag for the carriage. Please let me go. I need to pack shoes and dresses."

"Oh, all right. I am going to stay here. Don't take too long," replied Princess Marie aloud snobbishly, so everyone heard. "Come right back."

Upon walking out, she moved slowly out of the room, not wanting to call attention to herself. Instead of walking through the secret passage, she left through the doors because she wanted to investigate what the palace looked like after Versailles had been mobbed. Angelina felt that it was safe to walk the hallways now since the royal family announced that they were leaving. The palace was protected for now until after the royal family left for Paris. Once France's royal family did leave, and only after they left would the looters come to rob and vandalize Versailles. Angelina moved carefully and cautiously, so no one suspected her with the queen's jewels, or if anyone tried to harm her. The hallway walk interrupted her troubled thoughts of being a thief because of what she saw when she opened the doors to leave. Blood! Red covered, smeared parts of the hallway. A stench masked the odors of the stink of urine inside Versailles. It burned her nostrils. It was a new repulsive reek that made her belly queasy since it was made from puddles of blood that splattered across the floors.

Angelina used her hand to cover her nose and mouth from the repulsive smell. The hallways looked wet, painted with blood. Angelina held her breath, lifted, and adjusted her petticoats weighed down by the jewels, and ran before anyone could catch her, if in case anyone remained looking for royals to capture or kill. Versailles was in despair. Bodies had been carried away into unmarked graves. She found another secret door, and entered it to get away from the bloody floors.

When she entered Madame Royale's and her bedchambers on the ground floor that they had shared, she focused on packing. She was relieved that she remembered that her uncle's letter was hidden inside her diary already packed. Immediately, she packed her savings that she kept in a pair of silk stockings. Thank goodness, she thought, it was still there. She placed it on the bottom of her bag. Next, she rolled up her dresses, shifts, stays, chemise, and petticoats into the tapestry bag. She pulled out the jewels from underneath her petticoats and wrapped them up inside of the dresses that she planned on wearing once she got to America. She packed all her mobcaps, six pairs of silk slippers, placed one pair around the four sides, and two on top. She reached for her writing box that contained the quill pen ink, and powder to dry it. She wrapped it in the wool blanket, folded it in a square, and stuffed it on the top of her belongings, and tied it shut. She changed and dressed in her warmest dress, her heaviest wool coat, and the sturdiest pair of slippers.

Angelina looked around her bedchamber room for the last time. Flashbacks of all the wonderful times they had shared in their apartments flooded her sensitive mind. The books they read aloud to each other, the times they played with their dolls, and the nights they slept in each other's beds. It was unbelievable and horrifying to think her life with her best friend was all over. She couldn't understand how it had happened. Her life had been perfect, and now her world was shattered like broken glass. She was completely alone. Angelina knew that she would have to be brave and pick up the pieces of her life that was to be on her own.

She was determined to follow her plan, which comforted her. She was going to America to find Uncle Claude Savoy at this Mackinac Island in the Northwest Territory. She was getting out of France as fast as she could, but first, she had to get to Paris and exchange the jewels for money.

Angelina gathered her courage. She stepped out into the Marble Courtyard where masses of citizens were cheering. From a distance, she observed that the Black Guards and National Guardsmen held the angry mobs off. All the guards working together wore the new tricolor revolutionary cockade. She watched as General Lafayette forced his way forward with his sword in the air ready for any fight. She waited for her royal family to come out. Which carriage was the royal family being taken away in? Was it the carriage that she spotted by the main entrance door?

In the meantime, while waiting for the royal family to make their exit, she watched the servants tying trunks on top of the carriages. General Lafayette swung himself onto his horse that a groom brought forward to him. She raced toward the carriages, pushing past people so the princess could get to see her again. She rushed towards the carriages just in time to see the royal family, as they came out to the carriages that awaited them. The masses cheered even louder when they saw the king.

"Marie!" Angelina shouted her name above the shouting, cheering masses to be heard by the princess. Angelina caught up to her, and touched Princess Marie on the arm. Marie Therese twirled around. Angelina straightened up.

"Angelina! Come with us!" Madame Royale's eyes were pools of tears. She hugged Angelina, but instead of pulling Angelina into the carriage, she kissed her on the cheek, and the princess pushed her away. "You have to go, I know. You will always be with me. Take whatever you can in Versailles for money to get to America to find your uncle. Be safe and stay hidden until you get to America."

King Louis and Queen Marie Antoinette stepped into the first carriage. The queen held Louis Charles. Princess Marie stepped into the carriage last. The door shut, and the horses started up Grand Avenue de Paris. The following carriages carried the king's sister, other lower members of the royal family, and servants. The crowds surrounded the carriages on both sides of the road. Within half an hour, the infamous Marble Courtyard started to empty.

Chapter 6

Back inside Versailles, Angelina found that the looters hadn't found Queen Marie's bedchamber yet. Angelina knew that looters would soon come not wanting to miss destroying the queen' rooms and all that they held, but not before taking anything for themselves. There were still the slippers that the queen had not managed to put on, lying on the floor. Angelina came back for the big necklace. She wanted to know if Queen Marie had taken it. Yes! Queen Marie left it! The most significant necklace that the queen owned. The first time Angelina had come in to steal from her queen, she didn't think of stealing it. She never considered taking the biggest jewels for herself, of course, leaving them for Queen Marie to take with her when they left for Tuileries Palace, but there it was, The Diamond Necklace. King Louis the XV, who was the great king, grandfather to Louis XVI, had requested the necklace made to tempt the Comtesse du Barry. The grandfather king's mistress had gifted it to Marie Antoinette to bribe her, which she hoped would influence Queen Marie to befriend her. Queen Marie only told her husband that the necklace was to elaborate and showy for her to wear, but never wore it because she did not like the grandfather king's mistress. Oh my ███, she thought, I can't believe it's still here. No looters, Thank God!

She clutched it in her hands and carefully placed it across in her stay, covering her chest. It felt cold and pricked at her skin some, yet she could manage it since her life was at stake. She stuffed all the rest of the queen's jewelry in between her belongings in her bag. Next, she planned to find food for the trip to Paris. Hunger pains gnawed in her. Slowly and carefully, Angelina had to walk the hallways, looking for looters. Down in the kitchen, she spotted a few men leaving. Chef Francois looked up, shocked to see her standing next to him.

"Bonjour Chef," greeted Angelina. "Is there any food left?"

"Angelina, Oh my ███! Where have you been? Of course, you must be hungry. Yes, there is food still. We have meats, bread, cheese, and pastries. You must tell me where you have been?"

Angelina watched Chef Francois make her a plate of ham, cheese baguette, and a cup of hot chocolate for her. He slid it in front of her; she proceeded to answer his questions.

"I said my good-bye to the princess," she replied, trying not to cry, "and watched them leave. What has happened to you since they left?"

"I stayed hidden down here," he admitted, "after the yelling had calmed down. I went up to see what was going on. Everyone in the kitchen heard the announcement that the king and queen had surrendered to the peasants. I watched General Lafayette with his sword ready in the air for anyone who came to close to the royal family's carriage as he led them on horseback to Paris. Once I came back down here, I heard the masses of peasants trying to force their way into Versailles, but the palace guards and National Guardsmen would not let them in to loot the palace. Some managed to get in. I don't know what they took, but they haven't come down here so far. I am happy about that. They could come down still, so we are all taking what we can before they try to kill us. We have to be quick with our good-byes."

"Chef, do you think the royal family will ever be able to come back to their beloved palace?"

"I don't think so, Angelina. Versailles will become a museum of our noble past."

While he talked of his plans, Angelina glanced around the kitchen, reflecting on the special days she spent watching Chef Francois cook for the royal family. Often, she had secretly ventured into the hot, humid kitchen to watch Chef as he created culinary masterpieces. She remembered one time, how he was pressured by the king to impress an American man. Angelina reflected on the afternoons that she had carefully copied recipes down in her diary when she learned how to cook by studying how his dishes were created.

The most memorable moment in the kitchen was when she had met that one American that Chef had cooked for, Thomas Jefferson. He had sailed from a colony named Virginia. Thomas Jefferson was invited to Versailles to dine every Tuesday. While Thomas Jefferson was at Versailles, Angelina had met him in the kitchen when she had snuck down for a snack. He had been taking notes in a blank book, writing a few recipes, and drawing sketches of the kitchen at Versailles. Angelina remembered how nervous she was when he had asked for her name, what her job was, and how she liked living at Versailles. It was hard at first, she thought, to speak to him in his English language. She had learned English with the princess from her different governesses throughout their schooled years. It had been difficult with her strong, French tongue.

He was so tall, and so handsome with reddish-graying hair, dressed so clean. He looked like an aristocrat to her. They had become kindred spirits meeting in the kitchen. He taught her a little informal English. They had discussed favorite foods such as his first creamy dish of macaroni and cheese, crepes, chocolate éclairs, holiday recipes, and all kinds of worldly subjects. How sad she was when it was time for him to go back to America. He had just left France at the end of September from the port of Le Havre. He told her that he was taking home a noodle making machine, other French kitchen machines, French made copper pot and pans, copper made utensils, and what was learned at Versailles along with his Chef, James Hemmings. He had brought this black slave man with him special to France to learn to cook in the French ways. Thomas Jefferson was also going to grow French vegetables from the seeds he took back home and cook them in recipes on his plantation home that he called 'Monticello'.

It would be winter when she arrived in America. She wouldn't be able to travel to Mackinac Island without freezing to death. She recognized the fact that this was to be almost a year-long journey. Angelina realized that she would have to find employment somewhere to survive through the winter months, so that she wouldn't freeze to death. She would search for a ship, she thought, that landed in Virginia. Find Mr. Thomas Jefferson and work for him in his Monticello plantation home.

That would be the perfect plan. If she could find a ship that would take her to Virginia. She had her savings to live off of for food and lodging for now. It would be safer to use money. She wouldn't look like a thief giving away jewels, and possibly get robbed by real thieves, or arrested by the police. Once she arrived in Paris, she would sell off the jewelry, and that would be the money to pay for passage on a ship.

"Chef," Angelina interrupted," I am going to America."

"How do you think you will get there? Do you have enough money?"

"Yes, I have money that I saved." Angelina knew she was telling half-truths, but how could she confess that she had stolen from their queen. It was dishonorable, but now she had to fight for her life. She did not want Chef Francois to know her shame even though he had suggested it in the first place.

"I am determined to go to Mackinac Island, in the Northwest Territory to meet my uncle. I plan on taking a ship as soon as I can. I will be fine. I have packed for my journey to the New World," she stated, as she picked up her huge tapestry bag to show him. "I just need to pack some extra food."

"Angelina, please be safe on your journey. I can give you enough slices of ham, a dozen sausages, two baguettes, four bottles of the sweetest red wine from the king's cellar for the sweetest girl in France," he stopped to catch his breath. He could not hold back his tears of love for her. He stopped to hug her, and wiped his tears away while he tried to be brave for her. "And a wine opener to fill your bag. Save at least two bottles of wine for when you get to the New World to share with your uncle, or for yourself. When you drink your wine, think of me. I will pray for your safety to America. Stay at the best taverns, and you can buy bottles of wine there with your dinners along the way to drink with the wine I gave you. Be strong and carry the tapestry bag right, or it will break. You have to be careful of it. It carries all you have left to take into your new life.

"One thing before you go. When you arrive in America, you be sure to gain employment as a kitchen maid. You may not like it, but you will do well in servitude indoors. I have loved you as my daughter. You will always be in my prayers as you make the journey to find your uncle. May God keep you safe, mademoiselle."

"I have loved you like a father with all my heart," cried Angelina, she couldn't hold her secret from him. "I did take the jewels," and she pulled out from her tapestry bag two diamond rings and two diamond necklaces for him. "Take these, and I know you will be secure." In stunned silence, he took them from her, pulled her in, kissed her cheeks, and hugged her one last time.

Chapter 7

Angelina sobbed as she walked out of the royal courtyard, leaving her beloved Versailles forever. She was devastated that her life at Versailles was over. Angelina walked out of Versailles, looking back many times while she walked up Avenue de Paris until she couldn't see Versailles anymore. She stopped after two hours of walking to relax her aching feet. She used the wine opener, drank half a bottle of wine to refresh herself, two sausages, and ate half of a baguette from her food bundle. It will be too dark before arriving in Paris, she thought. It would be much safer to find a tavern outside of Paris to eat and rest to get her strength back after what she had been through the last day at Versailles. After hours of walking, Angelina was cold, exhausted, hungry, and her feet were hurting badly. She walked into a tavern that lured her in from the spicy aromas of meats roasting and fresh bread. Angelina gave the tavern keeper some money out of her savings for payment for a bed and food for the night. Her arms pained from having to carry her tapestry bag for hours and her legs cramped up on her from having walked most of the day. Her mind was tired from having to watch out for criminals waiting in the woods to ambush her. A hot bath in their bathhouse was offered to her, which she cheerfully accepted. It gave her body new strength as she relaxed her tired, aching muscles, and swollen feet. Once in her room, there was beef bourguigon, a warm baguette with butter, and an unopened bottle of wine that the tavern maid had brought up. She put the unopened wine bottle in her tapestry bag to save like Chef Francois had told her to do. She pulled out the bottle that she already opened, and drank a little of it with her supper. Later in bed, she gave in to a new fresh batch of tears from exhaustion and loneliness. Her dreams were filled with happy times at Versailles.

At daybreak, Angelina rubbed her sleep, crusted eyes open. While Angelina lay in bed, she discovered that for the first time in her life, no one summoned her. She was not comfortable with the silence. If she was at Versailles right now, she and the princess would be in their school time. Depressed, she sprang out of bed to fight off her sadness, opened the shutters, and checked the sky that was another gray autumn morning. The walk to Paris was going to be between four and six hours. Maybe if she jumped back to bed, pulled the blankets over her head, and prayed to God that

Versailles had never been attacked. Then, when she pulled back the covers, she would be back in Versailles with her best friend. She wished all of what had happened could have only been a nightmare. Was Princess Marie missing her? She had to focus, she thought, on herself now. However, she cried in sorrow, and she tried to tell herself that she can't torture herself with things that she couldn't change. She finished off the ham, four sausages, the other half of the baguette, washed it down with the rest of the bottle of wine, and left in the early afternoon for Paris.

Before dusk, Angelina arrived in Paris. She felt more energetic when she reached her destination because it was still daylight. Even though the bottom of her feet were covered in mud, the sun had come out the last part of her walk. It had been warm and wonderful, so it made the walk easier instead of trudging in mud. However, her body shivered from autumn breezes. Angelina was awe-struck when she looked up, and stared at the majestic stained glass rose window of Notre Dame. The shopkeepers' awnings were up, the smells of food, bread and wine coming out of the taverns welcomed her on her arrival. She made arrangements first to lodge and eat at the best tavern for dinner later that had the best smells coming out of it.

Before Angelina decided to pawn the jewels, she needed to get warm. She freshened up from her long trip. She ate two sausages, a chunk of baguette, and opened another bottle of wine to wash it down. Angelina couldn't wait to unload the heavy jewels that weighed on her.

Angelina boldly walked into a pawn shop,

"Salut Sir, I have a few rings, earrings, and necklaces that I wish to exchange for livres."

"Mademoiselle," he looked at her suspiciously, "Do you have these pieces with you?"

Angelina slowly pulled them out of her drawstring le sac, which she bought for the occasion. She placed three medium sized diamond necklaces, three diamond rings, and three pairs of diamond earrings on the countertop. She watched his eyes while he studied the jewels through an eyepiece. Angelina assumed that this must be the usual routine to make sure that they were real.

As he put down the last ring on the countertop, he smiled up to her, "These are real. Let me go in the back and pay you accordingly."

"Thank you, Sir. I am grateful for your kindness."

"You're welcome. I will be back with your money." He turned his back and walked to the back of the store. The money was nearly in her grasp.

Angelina was trembling with anticipation. Her hands were sweaty, and all she could do was pace the floor to help stop her jitters. While she waited, she heard a door shut. He must have to use a privy, she thought, or maybe the money was in another area possibly in the back room of his business. After what seemed like a long ten minutes, she started to wonder what was going on with him. She didn't like that it was taking too long. Angelina grabbed the jewels back off the countertop, putting them away in her drawstring le sac, and put it in her stay. Angelina didn't want to bring her tapestry bag since it was so heavy, and didn't want to lug it around. She thought it was safer in her tavern room. She listened for the door as it creaked open. Her heart jumped, she overheard footsteps: lots and lots of steps coming in from the back.

Suddenly, from behind the back door, four policeman ran to catch her with swinging swords. She ran out of the store. Breathing hard, she ran for her life in fear of the Bastille. Her lungs burning, Angelina found an alley with wooden barrels along the sides of the walls for garbage. She opened the lid of a barrel, jumped into it, and pulled the lid back on top. She listened for voices and feet run past the alleyway. Luckily, she thought, no one was in the alley to see her. She would have to wait until it was safe, and hopefully before anyone came out to dump more garbage into the barrel.

Chapter 8

By nightfall, she came out of the barrel and ran back to the tavern. Thank God, she prayed, that no one came into her tavern room to steal her tapestry bag. I don't think it is a good idea, she thought, to keep it in here while I am gone so much. I don't want to chance it, getting robbed in my room. She carried some onion soup, a fresh baguette, a cold mug of milk, and an unopened bottle of wine up to her room. I will save the wine, she thought, for another day.

Inside the bathhouse, she bathed in lavender water in the tavern's bathhouse to get the garbage smell off that lingered on her. She listened to the sounds of city chatter outside from the closed window when she climbed in the hot tub. Horses clip clopping and the wheels of carriages rolling over cobblestones, people talking while walking over the cobbles, and the ringing of the bells of Notre-Dame. Wound up, she was in deep thought as to where she would go next.

Half the night, Angelina had nightmares of the policemen with their muskets ready to take her away to the Bastille. Angelina slept in late, and ate the last four sausages, the other half of her last baguette, and the last half of the wine bottle that Chef Francois has given her. She had eaten all the food, but still had four bottles of wine. Two from what Chef had given her and the two she bought from the taverns. She would save them for special occasions or if she was starving, she decided, it would be easy to buy cheap food from street venders along the way until she could find a way to leave France.

Later that afternoon, she napped hard since the shock of leaving Versailles. Upon leaving the tavern, she wanted to explore to see what news the city told of the royal family. She took her tapestry bag with her since she trusted no one. She walked around Paris and walked to the Palais Royal. The Palais Royal was famous for shopping and entertainment. It was built with a huge public garden complex that was surrounded by the shopping arcades. It was one of the most valuable marketplaces for the aristocracy, middle classes, and lower orders of France to enjoy. Along the front facade, she passed shopping galleries of cafés, boutiques, bookstores, jewelry stores, refreshment kiosks of different flavors of lemonade, and museums.   One museum that she especially enjoyed walking through was a wax museum. Angelina loved the wax figures of King Louis XVI and Queen Marie Antionette. The likeness that was sculpted of them looked real, she thought, they were fantastic, bizarre, and sad to look at knowing that she would never see them again.

While she strolled around, she walked to the jewelry stores after she bought a lemonade. Angelina casually looked to see who behind the counter would look like the type who would help her.

Out of the corner of her eye, Angelina glanced down at a street boy sitting down, staring at her. The boy was tall and lean with thick brown wavy hair that was curly on top and cut around the ears. His eyes were brown, his face was handsomely chiseled, and his hands were rough and tanned from hard work. His britches were dingy brown, and his beige pheasant shirt was old and faded.

"You don't look like you belong here," the street boy said to her with a sarcastic tone.

"How would you know anything about me?" She snapped at him.

"I know your hands, and your face are pale and pink. A real commoner has hands and face tan and rough. I bet you have never done a hard day's work in your whole life. You walk like a noble's daughter."

"I am a servant girl out for the day," as she tried not to look at him and stuck her nose in the air, "on my day off."

"So what are you doing out with a tapestry bag? Looking for a place to rest for the night like a beggar girl?"

"It is none of your business!"

"You seem to be an interesting girl," he laughed at her spunk, "I am Jacque Beck. This is my little brother, Phillipe," as he pointed to him. "We came for the puppet shows. Why don't you relax and join us?"

"Why would I want to sit with you? You are a rude boy."

"What are you afraid of? I won't bite you."

"I am not afraid of you." And she sat down between the two dirty boys. She could see that they were brothers. The young one looked like a younger version of the oldest. "My name is Angelina Savoy. I am tired of wandering around," Angelina admitted, shocked by her courage to stand up for herself and how relaxed she was around him.

"Don't you have a family to go home to?" asked Jacque.

"No, my parents are dead. My father was a soldier who died in battle in America. My mother died when I was a baby."

"So you say," teased Jacque.

"I told you, I am a servant girl. What do you do? Beg day and night here at the Palais Royal for money?"

"No, we are apprentice shoemakers."

"So, you are tradespeople? Then, what are you doing on the streets? Isn't your mother wondering where you are?"

"We have no parents. Our parents passed away last winter. We come here for lemonade and entertainment."

"I'm sorry." They were not unlike her in that they both had lost parents. She felt especially sorry for the younger brother to lose one's parents so young. She didn't know her parents at all, so it didn't really hurt her like it would hurt someone who had actually made memories with their parents, knowing them growing up, and knowing what they sounded like. She softened to them in grieving for them. She found them interesting. "Where do you live now?"

"We sleep above Monsieur du Vance's shoe shop. Our father was a shoemaker. Before my father died, he bought our apprenticeship to the shoemaker for seven years for each of us. The shoemaker and his wife treat us as their sons. They don't have children of their own. We have to go now. The sun is going down. Would you like to come to supper, or do you have to get back to your noble's home?"

Angelina thought it better to let them go on without her, but hunger pained her. She could go back to the tavern, but the thought of safety indoors and food from another's home would be better. The police could still be looking for her and find her at the tavern that she was staying at.

Madame du Vance invited Angelina to stay the night after a wonderful dinner of roasted chicken, roasted potatoes with pan gravy, country bread, and a little red wine for her.

"It is too dark to be traveling the streets alone," agreed Monsieur du Vance, "at this time of night for a girl."

Monsieur du Vance insisted that she stay with them, "due to all the rioting because of our selfish king and queen, and the thieving that plagues the streets of Paris. Our country is so poor now due to the negligence of the king and queen."

It hurt Angelina to hear such things, but she could not argue with them. She decided to accept their invitation at their nagging for her to stay. It would be shocking to them, she thought, if they heard her stories having lived with the king and queen as a father and a mother. They had been good to her, even with all of France to look after. King Louis XVI had even been kind enough, she remembered, to give money to the Americans that helped them win their war for independence against the English king.

Chapter 9

Late in the night wide-awake, Angelina kept thinking of telling Jacque the truth of what had happened to her since leaving Versailles. She must not give in to her feelings, she thought, he may laugh in disbelief. Hundreds of scenarios tormented Angelina, if she told him the truth about herself and her journey. However, she had to find a pawn man, jeweler, or a tradesman who would give her money for the jewels of Queen Marie Antoinette. Jacque may know of someone, she thought, who could help her.

Angelina pulled back the sheets. She climbed out of bed and decided to take Jacque into her confidence. Angelina walked quietly to Jacque's room. In spite of her fears, she took a deep breath, turned the door handle, and tip-toed inside. Angelina froze when she shut the door. Her eyes adjusted to the moonlight in the room. Glancing between the two beds, she distinguished between the two boys. How was she supposed to start? Where would she start? At what point - at

Versailles, or when she was a young girl, or the day Versailles was attacked a few days ago.

Angelina debated with herself what she planned on saying when she woke him. He turned over, opened his eyes, and saw her. She sat down and put her finger to her lips.

"Shhh! It's only me, Angelina. Don't wake Philippe," she whispered. "I need to talk to you."

"Can't it wait until tomorrow? I have to get up early."

"I'm sorry, but I can't wait."

"Well," Jacque sat up. "What is it that can't wait?"

"I want to tell you the truth about me," Angelina whispered. "I am in danger. I have a secret. I have to get to America."

"What?"

"You see, I have to start at the beginning, the nobles I told you I worked for. They weren't just nobles. I served the royal family."

"Wait," replied Jacque dumbfounded. You are telling me that you were a servant to King Louis XVI and Queen Marie?" I know that they were taken to the Tuileries Palace as prisoners on house arrest two days ago."

Angelina put her hand over her mouth, and gasped in shock that he knew where they were imprisoned on house arrest.

"Yes. I hope they are fine since they still live in a palace. I wasn't just a servant girl. I am Princess Marie's best friend, or was. I was her companion, her under-governess."

"You were Madame Royale's personal servant?"

"Yes and No," retorted Angelina, "I was her best friend and the queen was a mother to me."

"So, what happened? Why are you not with them now?"

"I don't know if I can talk safely without anyone wanting to capture me."

"That's a little crazy don't you think. It's only you and me. And if you haven't noticed, Philippe doesn't talk. He hasn't talked since our parents died. The doctor said it was due to the tragic loss, but not to worry that Philippe will talk when he's ready to mourn our parents fully."

"Oh, I hope he opens up someday soon. I didn't notice."

"Philippe will be normal when time passes. Now, get back to the royal family. How are you not still with them?"

"I escaped the royal family and the rioters by stealing the queen's jewels and hid in a secret passageway inside the palace walls. Yesterday, I tried to exchange the jewels. The pawn man called the police on me while I waited for the money. Now, I am in hiding. I need to escape out of France to get to America. I have an uncle that lives on an island called Mackinac Island in the Northwest Territory in America. So that is where I am going."

Angelina swallowed hard. Jacque's eyes narrowed, questioning her story.

"You stole the queen's jewels. Are you serious?"

"Why would I lie about stealing from the queen?"

"Do you know if the police have followed you here? Have you led them here?"

"No, they don't know where I am. Maybe, the police have forgotten about me."

"I have an idea. You need to disguise yourself as a boy. We need to cut your hair, and you can borrow some of my clothes."

"I have only a little money left."

"Monsieur du Vance is friends to most of the tradesmen, citizens, and beggars in Paris. I think Monsieur du Vance can help you. I will talk to him about it, but I have one condition."

"What do you want? I will give you anything if you can help me trade these jewels?"

"Pay the passage for Philippe and me to sail to America."

"What about your apprenticeship with the shoemaker?" Can Monsieur du Vance let you go?"

"He will, or we will run away with you. I want to go to America. I can make shoes in America. I have made shoes since I was seven years old. I am fourteen. I am my own man. Philippe and I will open our own shop in America away from the troubles of France."

"Will the shoemaker survive if you leave?"

"Of course, he has had his shop for many years. Monsieur du Vance only took us in as a favor to our parents when he knew that my parents were dying from Yellow Fever, so we would be well taken care of. He felt it his responsibility to my father to further our learning in our trade. I will talk to him tomorrow. I know he will give back to Philippe and me some of the money that our father gave to him for keeping us because he is a good man. Do we have a deal?" he asked as he put his hand out.

"Deal," she avowed, as she shook his hand.

"You know you are going to have to make up a fake name to be a boy," Jacque pointed out. "What do you think you want for a boy name?"

"I think something that starts with an A. I think I would be more attentive to it, if someone called me out. I like Alexandre. Its sounds like my name, Angelina."

"Sounds right! Alexandre, I like it!"

At breakfast, Jacque announced to the shoemaker about wanting to sail to America with Angelina. Much to Angelina's surprise, Monsieur du Vance agreed that France was in turmoil. He decided that it might be better if his friend's sons went to America because of all the violence in France. The shoemaker's wife had her doubts, but she knew every boy had to find his own path.

Jacque turned to Angelina, "You are safe among friends."

In Monsieur du Vance's home, Angelina was sure no harm would come to her. Everyone at the table was wide-eyed and taken aback, as Angelina confessed to them of her life in Versailles, having lived with the royal family, the rioters that attacked Versailles, and how she stole Queen Marie Antionette's jewels to finance her journey to Mackinac Island in the Northwest Territory of America.

The shoemaker, his wife, and Philippe stared at her, astonished by her story.

"Can we see these jewels, so we know what we are trying to sell?" asked Monsieur du Vance.

"Yes," said Angelina. "Do you think you can help me find a buyer?"

Everyone held their breath. Angelina slowly pulled out all the jewels from her tapestry bag and laid them on the table. Everyone was silent in shock of the dazzling beauty from the jewels in rings, earrings and necklaces that had been laid before them.

"How long do you think it will take to find a tradesman to sell the jewels?"

"I know a few good men," Monsieur du Vance offered, "who could help you. We will have to be careful of policemen who are looking for you. Let me speak with these men. We will find out who we can trust."

Two days later, Angelina cut her hair short. No one would have guessed from her appearance that Angelina was nothing more than a handsome boy of thirteen years old. It will be nice, she thought, not have to wear a mobcap for a while. Jacque managed to buy her some boy clothes, a wool coat, red caps, stockings, boots, and shoes for winter was closing in. Angelina stared at her new hair in their small hand mirror. She felt insecure and awkward in her new attire as a boy.

"You have to wear this Phrygian cap," Jacque educated her about having to wear the red liberty cap. "Everyone in France is wearing them now. We will blend in better in public with France's revolutionaries. It is the hat of the people, and it's worn pinned with the tricolor cockade on it like this," showing her as he pinned a tricolor cockade on the side. "It shows that you support the revolutionaries."

Angelina had to agree, but she felt like a traitor to the royal family. In the meantime, they waited to hear word from Monsieur de Vance. She was finishing sewing the remainder of the jewels into the lining of her wool coat when the shoemaker walked through the door.

"I have good news. It happens tonight. I have found the perfect man to help. This man is a tradesman. He sells French wares to an American mercantile company. I think he has inside connections to this mercantile company that I have spoken with that carries stowaways for a high price. He wants us to come after nightfall when most of France is sleeping in their beds."

Monsieur du Vance and Angelina met the tradesman late that night. Jacque and Philippe stayed behind with Madame du Vance to keep her safe in case the policemen came looking for Angelina there. They never knew if their neighbors could have been watching them in the wee hours of the night. Before they left, Angelina placed the Phrygian cap on, concealed the jewels in a drawstring le sac under her belt, and some in the front fall of her undergarments. It would be too dangerous to walk around with a bag in case they were robbed, or if the policemen questioned them on why they were out late in the night.

"Salut, garcons," greeted the tradesman in the back of his shop, "the shoemaker has told me your dilemma. You have the most interesting story that I have ever heard."

"Thank you, sir, for your kindness in offering your services."

"Don't mention it. I would kill to see the queen's jewels just for my own curiosity."

The tradesman speechless, under candle light marveled at the shimmering, sparkling glitz of a heavy diamond necklace in his hands.

"This necklace," said Angelina, as she pointed to the elaborate diamond necklace with the three loops of diamonds and four diamond-studded metallic bows that hung down four strands of diamonds, "was first given to Madame du Barry from grandfather King Louis XV to tempt her, and it did win her over. She was the grandfather king's mistress, which everyone knew in Versailles from what I heard. It was a gift to Queen Marie Antoinette from Madame du Barry after she married King Louis XVI. You see the grandfather king's mistress was trying to get into the queen's good graces. Queen Marie would never wear it on purpose because she never liked the grandfather king's mistress."

"You are a treasure, mademoiselle" he said since he knew that she really wasn't a boy. "You are filled with all kinds of information for me. I am at your bidding. My cousin is married to a sailor that works for the American merchant company that accepts stowaways for a price. I do a profitable business with them. The company's name is Roderigue, Hortalez, and Company. They have ports in Pennsylvania, Massachusetts, and Virginia. Where did you plan on landing in America, mademoiselle?"

"Sir, I would like to land in Virginia?"

"Very good," replied the tradesman, and he wrote a note on a small piece of parchment. "I will help you get there. This note, you must not lose," as he handed it to her.

"The note has the address of my cousin in Nantes. It informs her that you are my friend, whom I have given over to her, and in her care until her husband returns. They will get you on the ship that is going to Norfolk, Virginia."

The kind and generous tradesman produced a drawstring le sac, heavy with gold coins and sols. Angelina peeked in and clutched it to her chest, taking a deep breath, thankful that her journey was getting closer now that she could touch the livre in her possession. She put the note into the drawstring purse.

"It will help get you settled wherever you decide you want to live in America. Bonsoir, au revoir, mademoiselle. May God bless you and keep you safe on your journey."

Chapter 10

The trio started on horse and cart provided by the shoemaker. They encountered no problems through the counties of Orleanais, Maine, Anjou, and into Brittany. In twelve days' time, they arrived in the port city, Nantes. The sun was out, but the weather was cold and crisp. Along with the stench of fish that lingered in the air. The small party disposed of the horse and cart. Angelina with her tapestry bag and each with their new, big leather travel bags in their hands were ready to explore the city. Angelina was happy that her load felt lighter with her food, wine, and clothes. She could carry her belongings easier with no concerns of the handles breaking on her travel bags. One hand held onto the tapestry bag with two bottles of wine, wool blanket, and her clothes in it. The other held onto the new leather bag with the other two bottles of wine and food along with clothes on top, and the remaining jewels in between both bags. They searched on the dirt roads for the apartment from the address on the tradesman's note.

"The ocean breeze," declared Philippe "makes me feel better!"

Jacque and Angelina perked up.

"That's good, Philippe," Jacque encouraged him. "Breath it in! It's good for the lungs!"

There was a celebratory air between the two since Phillipe finally spoke. The three adventurers watched the seagulls overhead circling the shore in the distance. The little breezes relieved their senses and strengthened their spirits. However, they grew anxious the longer they searched until they found the residence.

Angelina flushed and knocked on the door. Her body had begun to jitter with worry.

"Who is knocking?" A gentleman's voice shouted on the other side of the door.

"Pardon sir," Jacque called out, "we are looking for Madame du Tillet? I have a note from the tradesman in Paris, your cousin."

Suddenly, a young gentleman opened the door.

"Get in here quick. No one needs to hear you shouting in the streets."

The trio stepped in before the man changed his mind.

"Give me the note," he stated with a rude, uninviting tone, while he locked the door.

With her right-hand shaking, Angelina dropped her bags carefully on the floor, handed the most handsome man that she had ever seen, the note from the inside pocket of her wool coat that she wore heavy with the jewels sewn inside. She wanted to take off her red liberty cap to scratch the painful itching of her sweaty scalp while she waited to see if the man of the house would accept them into his home, but couldn't risk getting caught if the man recognized that she was a girl. In the end, she just scratched hard at it with the Phrygian cap on while she tried to act casual.

"I am Madame's husband. So you want to know if I can smuggle you three into Virginia, is it?"

"Yes, Sir," answered Angelina in a husky voice. "My name is Alexandre." It would be safer, she thought, just to tell him right away what her new name was. He was so handsome, she thought, with his red hair, baby face, and muscles.

"You are lucky the ships are in. They are ready to embark back to America before the winter sets in. How many livres do you have?"

So saying Monsieur du Tillet turned away, as a black-haired young woman walked out of a back room, hobbling as if she was drunk.

"How is little Victor?" he looked up at her from reading the note.

"He is sleeping, but still feverish," replied the distressed woman.

"Your cousin has sent us some kids who want to stowaway to America."

"Oh, I'm sorry. I didn't notice you three," said Madame du Tillet. "Our son is ill, and I have been up most of the night. How is my cousin?"

"Very well," Jacque answered, "he wishes you well. My name is Jacque," and that is my brother, Pierre."

Monsieur du Tillet cut in, "Do you have enough livre for the captain?"

"I have enough," Jacque answered, "for all three of us."

Angelina had given Jacque a drawstring le sac with the money it. He was the oldest of the three of them, so it made sense that the money given out should come from him.

"Good answer," he winked. "I wouldn't tell anyone what my sac was either."

"It will cost two Louis d'ors from each of you."

"That will be fine," Jacque replied.

It was cheaper, Angelina thought, than she imagined it would be.

Angelina spoke up, acting with a low throaty voice. "When do the ships plan on departing?"

"In a fortnight, we just arrived. The ships have to have time to load their new cargo. It is to be the last run of the season. I will speak to the Captain tomorrow. I will ask him to transfer me to the Virginia ship, the *Victorious*. I have not yet seen Virginia. You all can call me by my first name, Pierre. We don't have luxurious accommodations.

There is only the attic, but we have blankets to keep you warm."

"Just treat us as if we were working with you on the mercantile ship," Jacque spoke up. "We will help you carry cargo on the ship and row with you. If you will only feed us, there is nothing we will not do for you."

"We will care for you as if you were family," Madame du Tillet replied.

"You three are our guests," stated Monsieur du Tillet, "until we embark on the *Victorious.*"

Madame du Tillet treated them to a supper of fresh fish fried in butter in a pan over the hearth fire with fried potatoes, fresh bread, and wine. After hours of chatting, eating, getting to know each other, the party separated to go to their beds. I am so happy that I remembered to bring a wool blanket, she thought, or I would be freezing all night.

The following morning, the three found fisherman's clothes had been donated to them by Pierre.

"You two are fine," said Pierre, as he checked over Jacques and Philippe. "Your hands and face are too white," he said as he inspected Alexandre. "I tanned my sails already. There is some of the substance left that I have. It won't burn your skin, so rub your face and hands all over with it. It will work to disguise you."

Angelina took the handsome sailor's advice. The result gave the appearance of a boy whose face and hands were bronzed by long term exposure to the hard work of ocean and air.

"You will pass off as a sailor now," Pierre affirmed, while he walked around inspecting her. "I shall say that you are a young sailor transferred from another French port.

And so the week passed. During the week, they kept house for Madame du Tillet. Pierre had succeeded in asking the Captain, if he was willing to take them to America by the upcoming week. She was so excited, she could hardly wait. At times, she enjoyed thoughts, about sailing with Pierre and how nice it would be to be with his red-haired handsome self. Angelina respected that he was married and had a child, but still she enjoyed the fact that they would know each other for a little longer.

Just as Angelina had come back from her daily walk, she found the woman of the house in tears.

"Madame du Tillet, what is wrong? Is there anything I can do to help you?"

"My son is dying," Madame du Tillet exclaimed, red-faced and swollen from crying all afternoon. "His fever is getting worse. He is coughing so hard that he can't breathe. He is gasping for air, and he's crying. The crying just makes everything worse.

We can't afford to pay for a doctor to give him medicine. I am scared for my son's life."

Jacque and Philippe were out with Monsieur du Tillet buying clothes, Angelina took charge.

"I am going to get a doctor. Do not worry about the cost. I am going to take it upon my shoulders. See if you can get him to eat or drink something before, I return."

Immediately, Angelina ran the streets to find a doctor. She found him lazy until she laid a gold coin on his table. When she and the doctor returned, Pierre, Jacque, and Philippe were there with soup, bread, and wine to refresh her.

The doctor had quickly come out with a severe expression on his face.

"Victor has the croup. You need to boil pots of water immediately and get some heat and humidity in this home to loosen up the phlegm." The doctor handed her a dark colored bottle, "Madame, empty this bottle of Ipecac continuously little by little all through the night. I have already given him some. Victor needs to sip on it all night. It will help bring up the phlegm, so that he will cough it out. You need to change his bed linens and his clothes immediately. I will come back early tomorrow morning to check on him."

Once the doctor departed, Angelina confided to Madame du Tillet in Victor's room that she was a girl, revealed the truth of her real name, and revealed that she was an educated girl who knew how to nurse sick children. She kept it a secret from Madame du Tillet that she had learned a little about a few medicines including Ipecac from the doctors who had nursed the royal family's sickly sons. Both of them nursed little Victor all night. It had been a long, scary night when around one o'clock in the morning Victor coughed up the last of the phlegm, and his fever broke. Madame du Tillet kept Angelina's secret from her husband as a favor to Angelina for paying for the doctor.

The doctor returned in the morning, looking forward to another gold coin from Alexandre. Before the doctor left, he reassured the family that Victor was going to recover now that he had coughed up the phlegm.

The last day in France had finally arrived, and it had been arranged for the trio to leave France. Pierre was to row the three stowaways around midnight, so that the watchmen wouldn't catch them.

"We owe you for saving Victor's life," said Madame du Tillet to Angelina, as Monsieur du Tillet had brought in two leather trunks that sat on the floor by the door. "Thank you for your help, or my son could be dead. Pierre and I bought two leather trunks for your belongings for the ship from the money you gave us. One trunk is for the brothers, and the other trunk is you, Alexandre," winking at her.

"They will be the best to travel with on the ship. I have a bundle of food for you three and a bottle of wine for each of you to help keep your strength up on your journey to America. I will keep you in my prayers that you arrive to the New World safely with my husband, and the good Lord keep you safe all the rest of your days."

The port town was quiet and scarce a sound was heard throughout the streets as the moon was high in the sky. The only voices that echoed were from the drinkers in the taverns and the drunks that had made their way outside for some fresh air.

Under the cover of darkness, Pierre rowed out into the deep water. They pulled up the oars and drifted for a half an hour until they saw a ship blink a light three times.

"That is the signal. That is the *Victorious*."

In a few minutes, the rowboat reached the side of the ship, a rope was tossed to them, and the rowboat was lifted up with its passengers and their trunks. The Captain and the sailors patted their backs, shook hands, and cheerfully greeted the stowaways. By lantern lights, they were guided to their bunks with their belongings.

Their business could wait till the morning for it had been a long night. There would be plenty of time to attend to the business of payment for passage, for it was only the beginning of a long voyage that awaited them.

Chapter 11

"Which one of you has the livre for me?" Captain Adolphe bellowed, as he lit up his porcelain tobacco pipe. Angelina observed his unique white porcelain tobacco pipe that was painted red across the top with a rose flower spray on the outside of the bowl, and the hand carved, mahogany-stained wood mouthpiece. They waited for him to finish his smoking. "Let's see the money before I show you where you are to hide in what we have constructed for you."

The three friends steadied themselves to the swaying of the ship while they tried to keep from throwing up their small breakfast of strong coffee with sugar that they sipped on while they choked down biscuits with butter and orange marmalade.

Coffee for Angelina was something that she would have to get used to drinking. Coffee was popular in Versailles, so she was familiar with the smell and tastes of a few that she had tried. Too bitter of a drink, she thought, she couldn't drink it every day like some people did.

Over the next few months, Angelina was to find out that her diet was to consist of drinking coffee and vinegar shrubs. Instead of water, they were to drink weak beer with their meals.

"Tillet, stay with your shipmates! It is a small ship, garcons," the Captain pocketed his pipe, and removed his Captain's hat to scratch his balding head. "There will be times when you will have to stay hidden from the French Navy when we get near forts. I have to tell you two," as he pointed to Angelina and Philippe, "to hide on the bottom of the ship below the cargo and casks. It is tight, but you should be comfortable. We will be searched before we leave port. Once we get underway into the Atlantic, you will be free to roam on occasion.

"And you," he pointed to Jacque, "you are on my list of shipmates, so you will be able to work with the rest of the crew and fit in where need be."

"I am at your service, Captain."

"We are not afraid to go below and stay hidden, Captain," said Angelina, with a bold manly air. "My name is Alexandre. We are grateful that you took us on, and ready to put in our share of work on the ship."

"That's part of your payment, of course," Captain Adolphe smirked. He reached for his pipe, and puffed on it using his metal lighter.

Jacque pulled out the drawstring le sac and handed the captain the gold coins. "My name is Jacque, and that is my brother, Phillipe."

"Very well," he said joyously, as he pocketed the money. "Take them below! Master at Arms!" Captain Adolphe ordered, the Master-at-Arms took over, and the Captain puffed on his pipe.

"Let me show you to your hiding place. Bring your things," ordered the Master-at-Arms. "It will take us about fifteen minutes to close it up again."

The hatch was lifted, and the group climbed down into the hold of the ship that was full of crates and kegs to within three feet of the deck.

Captain Adolphe handed his Master-at-Arms a lantern.

"Follow my man," bellowed the Captain, "you have to crawl on your hands and knees!"

They followed the Master-at-Arms until they were close to the bulkhead that divided the hold from the forecastle. Three feet from this was a vacant space.

"Give my man your hands," Captain Adolphe shouted down to them. "He will lower you down! Your feet will touch the bottom. I have had hay put there for you to sit and sleep on."

The two were lowered down. They found themselves in a dark space that was six feet long and two feet wide. Angelina knew she was on the bottom when she felt fresh hay on the floor of the ship, and around it was crates. One side was formed by the bulkhead, on the other there were kegs. Five feet from the bottom, a wood beam was nailed to the bulkhead. Next, the cabin boy handed down to the Master-at-Arms a few short beams; he fixed them at one end resting on the beam, and the others in the space between the crates and kegs.

"These are to form the cover for a roof. I am going to head up now," The Master-at-Arms informed them. "We are going to put four tiers of kegs on these beams that will fill it up to level with the other kegs above. You will have sufficient air. I will leave the hatchway open. Are you content?"

"Completely," Angelina answered, yet Philippe was quiet. She sensed that the thought of the small dark space might have scared him. She reached her hands out in the dark empty space to find him to comfort him in the dark. Meanwhile, the crates and kegs positioned in their places were restacked and placed accordingly. All the stacks of cargo were made even and leveled when they heard Pierre holler out to the Captain,

"Captain, a gunboat is approaching out of port."

The Captain stood on the top deck with Jacque trailing behind him, ordered the sails to be lowered, as he puffed on his porcelain pipe. In a few tense minutes, the gunboat was side by side with the ship, and a new threat was on board.

Angelina laid down on her back on the soft hay as she tried to relax, yet frozen with fear. She tried to hear what was happening up on the top deck. Would she and her friends be found? Would they be imprisoned in the Bastille?

"Captain, I need to see your papers," the Lead Navy Officer ordered. He was followed by six of his men who had climbed on board with him, "and your list of crew members."

"They are both right here," the Captain said as he brought the lists out from inside of his vest pocket. "The list of my men and the list of cargo," he paused to puff his pipe. "The Commissary at Nantes inspected and placed his seal to it."

"Line up men! We shall call your name off the list!" The Navy Lead Officer announced.

The men did as told, and the Lead Officer bellowed out last names out of order to catch any stowaway.

"All is good with your men, Captain. Now, I need to examine your ship by my orders to see that you have no stowaways."

"Carry on! The *Victorious* has nothing but cargo set for America." Captain Adolphe openly laughed at him because he knew he was secure in knowing that he would never get caught, and he paused as he puffed his pipe,

"The hatch has been taken off for you, as you can see to save you time."

The six officers and the Lead Navy Officer searched the cabins and forecastles, and then descended down into the hold. Three lanterns were handed down to the men in teams of two. Phillipe fainted from fear of being caught while Angelina still laid on her back, held her breath, and she covered her mouth with both hands.

"All clear, sir," stated one of the young officers to the Lead Officer.

The others searched down around the crates and kegs.

"Make sure you move and shift some cargo!" ordered the Lead Navy Officer. "Make sure all is solid!"

Several crates were rearranged from their position, and some of the second tier was also shifted. The Lead Officer stomped around with his right foot making sure all was solid underneath too. Everyone on ship held their breath, until the Lead Navy Officer made his announcement,

"I think that your ship is secure to sail on now, Captain Adolphe. Your sailors can stow the cargo as it was. Au revoir, Captain, I wish a good voyage to you and your men. I hope you have a safe passage through calm and steady waters."

By the time the Lead Navy Officer and his men climbed into their gunboat, the Captain had given orders to raise the sails, and he puffed on his pipe.

95

The *Victorious* sailed quickly out of port leaving France in a trail of foam behind her. As soon as the gunboat was safely out of distance, Captain Adolphe gave direct orders to Pierre and Jacque to go below and check on the status of his stowaways.

"Are you two all right in there?" Pierre shouted.

"Yes," answered Angelina, "I am fine, but Philippe has fainted. He fainted when he heard them come down. I am sure all he needs is fresh air."

Angelina lifted Phillipe to Pierre, threw him over his shoulder to climb up, and get Phillipe some fresh air. On the top deck, a water-soaked cloth was handed to Angelina. She placed it on Phillipe's forehead. With the cloth and the fresh air, Philippe quickly recovered.

"Phillipe, we're safe," Jacque told him. We've left France forever!"

Watching the twilight colors of painted pinks and purples, and blues of the sunset sky, the *Victorious* sailed out into the open ocean.

Angelina, Jacque, and Philippe stayed out on the top deck looking out on the Atlantic. Each lost in their private thoughts until the bell rang for supper.

Angelina would always cherish her memories of the Palace of Versailles with France's royal family and Chef Francois. She would carry her memories of them with her forever.

She hated that she had left the princess. Angelina had felt fortunate that they had said their good-byes with hugs and farewell tears. She was on now on her way, and looking forward to meeting her uncle in America.

Chapter 12

Settling in for the night, the sailors celebrated with songs, dance, stories, food, and wine. The music and laughter relaxed everyone onboard for the long voyage. Angelina found her bed in the dark where the crew slept in the forecastle. Angelina found it difficult to sleep. The constant rising and falling of the ship, the snores of the other sailors around her, and the smell of the sailor's body odors made her feel sick.

At first light, Angelina was on the top deck away from the foul smell down below. The fresh winds made her feel refreshed. However, seasickness took hold of her, on and off for most of the day. Most of the time, she felt like she could vomit at any moment. Right away, Philippe suffered from severe seasickness. Jacque took care of him. Angelina tried to hide the fact from the crew that she had been sick all week until it got worse, out when the *Victorious* sailed into the dark, deep waters of the North Atlantic.

The crew laughed at Alexandre when they watched him puke over the side of the ship, and the

Captain laughed like a big joke to himself when he heard the news from his men because he knew one of them would get the seasickness.

Angelina ended up sick in bed over the next three days. Jacque stayed strong while attending to his brother and Angelina. Seasickness left her body chilled from the cold sweat and her mouth dry. Angelina's diet consisted of brined beef, salt pork, weak beer, and ship biscuits, or others called them hardtack what she could keep down. She slept on and off dreaming of nights in Versailles. She dreamed of the days when clothed in silk dresses trimmed with ruffles of lace for the glamourous balls at Versailles, admiring herself in the Hall of Mirrors. The ballroom overflowed with crystal candlelit chandeliers, gold statues, and glowing candlelit sconces. Princess Marie and herself watching everyone dressed in their finest, wearing their diamonds and jewels, and powdered wigs. They learned how the women swayed their fans, flirted with the men, and how the women danced with the men. She and the princess eating as many pastries they could get away with until their bellies hurt.

By week's end, Angelina could finally sit up although feeling shaky. Her skin felt sticky and wet from the sweat that had saturated her body. She climbed up out of bed slowly to wash herself. Jacque helped her to the top deck for some fresh air.

When Angelina was getting better, she found out that Philippe was getting sicker. Phillipe was worse off with fever and wasn't eating. Jacque tried to keep water in him, as Philippe kept vomiting. Angelina and Jacque took turns nursing him back to health. Angelina was still trying to get her appetite back. The smell of the cook's meals assaulted her senses. Angelina knew she had to eat. She had to get her strength back to help Jacque with the duties he had on board the *Victorious* and take care of his sick brother.

Gradually, Angelina managed to recover fully. Her hands were full keeping up with the duties on board. Within earshot, from time to time, she heard Captain Adolphe bellowing out orders. Angelina wanted to stay out of his way as much as possible.

"There's a storm brewing, heed my words!"

That night, massive swells of waves crashed against both sides of the *Victorious*. Captain Adolphe barked orders to Angelina and Jacque,

"Stay below with the young one! He needs you two more than we do!"

Angelina had been relieved at not having to deal with the storm and keeping the sails fastened down. She was afraid she would have been thrown overboard. The ocean sprayed and seeped down through the wood planks down onto their beds. Soon, it seemed as if buckets of freezing water had covered the floorboards. In an hour, the forecastle was flooded.

Angelina did her best to hold onto the side of her bunk while she tried fighting the painful feelings of her frozen, wet little body as the ship violently rocked from side to side. Suddenly, she fell and landed face first stunned. Angelina was thrown under the bottom bunk of one of the beds. Trapped, Angelina held her breath. She tried to pull her body out, and up for air. She held her breath, yet, her nostrils burned from the salt water. When the ship finally rocked the other way, Angelina quickly crawled out from under the bed. Jacque grabbed onto her shirt and heaved her up to stand, so she could hold onto the sides of the other bunks.

"Angelina, I thought I almost lost you," exclaimed Jacque.

"I'm all right," she replied, while she shivered.

Climbing back into her bunk, she wrapped herself in her wool blanket, and held onto the sides of her bed. She tried to stay balanced to the rocking of the ship until her knuckles turned white and the storm subsided. Angelina finally settled into slumber when the storm died down. The last sound she heard was of the sailor's coming down to their bed after a long scary night. She dreamt of walking around the vast gardens on the backside of Versailles, and sailing in a little sailboat that floated down the Grand Canal lined with trees, statues, and fountains from the middle of the gardens to the back of the gardens.

Four hours later, everyone was on deck checking the damage from the storm. Angelina watched over Philippe while Jacque stayed up on deck with the other sailors. Angelina feared for Philippe. He seemed to look grayer hour by hour.

"Go get my brother," said Philippe hoarsely.

"Why? I am here with you to keep you company."

"Please go get Jacque. I don't feel good. I feel funny."

Angelina ran out and hollered out on the deck, "Jacque! Jacque, come quickly!"

Jacque ran down below, pushing Angelina aside down to the ground. It was just the two of them by the boy's side.

"What is it, Philippe?"

"I am tired and feel funny. I don't think I am going to make it to America."

"Don't be silly, Philippe. We are going to America. We are going to have our own business making shoes. We are going to be our own men, you will see. Just take a nap. This will pass, you will get better."

"No, I'm not. I am going to be with Father and Mother. I love you, Jacque. Angelina, I loved you like a sister. I will look after you two in heaven." Philippe closed his eyes forever.

By sunset, Philippe's body was wrapped up in a blanket and secured with a rope around it. Jacque and Pierre lifted his tiny body, and carried him up on the top deck for the funeral.

Above the ship's sails, the sky was filled of a purple twilight. Far ahead in the distance the sunset sky shone like it had been painted pink as a great rose window to welcome Phillipe into God's great cathedral.

Every sailor lined up alongside the top deck shedding tears for a lost little one who would never know the joys of adulthood.

Captain Adolphe gave the eulogy and said a few prayers. When the Captain finished, he lit up his porcelain tobacco pipe. Angelina cried quietly while his body was cast overboard. She wept for her friend's loss of his dear, sweet, little brother. Angelina couldn't stop crying. She had known him only for a short time, but she felt that he had been her little brother too that she had lost.

Chapter 13

F ive weeks later still mourning Philippe, Captain Adolphe sent a message to Angelina and Jacque to dine with him that night. They could never refuse the captain's order. The meal was a simple one from the galley of roasted chicken with roasted potatoes, peas, hardtack and red wine. The roasted chicken was a treat after months of an unsteady diet of brined beef, salted pork and salted cod. The captain silently studied their behavior, and he lit up his porcelain tobacco pipe.

"Now, you two have to be strong for the little one you lost. It would do you two no good, if you failed him and died from starving yourselves from grieving over him. Life is what you make it. You have to go on living in spite of what life throws at you. You two still have your fortunes to make. We will be arriving soon, and you need to have your heads clear for landing in the New World. I suggest you two find farm people when we land in Virginia.

"Farmers take people in for the night, if you help with the work on their farms. Treat them good, and they will be useful to you. They may look like simple people. They are far from being simpletons. Farmers are the hardest working sort of people I have met. To live on the same piece of land and live by the seasons is a stable person. Never knowing what Mother Nature will throw at them. I tell ya, they are strong and their wives and children are too! Without ever leaving their homes," he chuckled, and he relit and puffed his porcelain tobacco pipe. "The farmers know all the gossip from what their wives hear in the settlement and bring back home to tell their happy husbands.

"In the next few days, you two will be off this ship. We are to sail into the Chesapeake Bay and sail into the town port in Norfolk, which is where we will land. Our buyers are waiting for us in the city. You two will have to leave at night when our friends in Virginia will signal to us that it is safe for you two stowaways. When you land, ask around for the friendliest tavern. Then, find the nearest farmers around. Where may I ask, do you want to go to find your fortunes in America?"

"I have an uncle that lives in the Northwest Territory that is waiting for me, sir."

"I am going to own my own shoemaking business."

"Good! Good! It looks as if you have goals in mind for yourselves! I think for you two; your journey will be a long one. I hear this winter is to be a long, bitter, cold one. You two should find some kind of work around Norfolk until spring."

"Thank you for your advice, Captain Adolphe," said Angelina, acting as Alexandre with her throaty, husky voice. "We planned on finding work over the winter in the city to help finance my journey northwards in the spring."

"Smart thinking lad," nodded Captain Adolphe. "Do you have many livres left?"

"I have some," Jacque answered for them politely, yet, on guard.

"Well, I suggest we make a trade. I have some New World currency, and I am going to need livre when we head back to France."

"Thank you, Captain," said Jacque. "I would like that very much. That is very kind of you."

Secretly, Angelina was much relieved that she wouldn't have to pass out any more jewels in order to survive.

Captain Adolphe gave them each a nip of brandy ending their visit. After warm good-byes, Angelina, back in her bunk, wondered what she would say to Monsieur Thomas Jefferson when she met him.

Four nights later, the moon was bright like a lantern in the night sky, Captain Adolphe signaled three times to the shore. The signal came back right away that their friends saw the ship on the port settlement's shore.

The signal meant it was time for the stowaways to depart, and Angelina was ready wearing her wool coat with the jewelry in it and her Phrygian cap to keep warm. Heartfelt good-byes were spoken to the crew, and Angelina thrilled when Pierre kissed her on the cheek and hugged her good-bye. Jacque grabbed their trunks and jumped into the bateau, or French rowboat that was taking them to the shore. Angelina climbed in the rowboat. Within half an hour, they were in the harbor of Norfolk, Virginia.

Hidden by darkness, they floated into the harbor that was encircled by trees, the port, and two-story wooden and stone buildings along the shore. It was hypnotizing staring at all the square windows glowing by candle light in the dark. There was an excitement in the air to see so much hustle and bustle of a prosperous city so late at night on the water. She was so surprised at the many different kinds of sail boats, canoes, tenders, bateaus, and schooners that were anchored by each other.

"Thank you, Father God!" Angelina muttered under her breath. It was so cold that they could see their breaths, but she felt more alive than ever.

The two of them found shelter in the best, most expensive tavern they located just in time as little whisps of snow fell lightly on their first American night. Dropping their trunks by the door, they decided that tomorrow they would find a farm nearby, and find out how far Thomas Jefferson's Monticello home was. She prayed that Thomas Jefferson would remember her while Jacque started a little fire in the tavern room's fireplace with wood that was left for them.

By midnight, they put on their nightclothes, they planned what their jobs were for the next day, and settled in their beds. Their bodies finally at two o'clock in the morning, surrendered to sleep after an adventurous night.

They awoke to a freezing cold room since the fire had died out. They purposely stayed at their current tavern because it offered a bathhouse, so they could have the biggest bubble bath after months of living on a ship. They threw away their filthy, foul smelling ship clothes and wool coats. They bathed, and put on the clean clothes they had saved for when they arrived in the New World.

Angelina felt so happy to be back too normal since the tragic day the marketplace peasant women had marched to Versailles so long ago. She felt relieved not having to be Alexandre anymore, hiding from the policemen who chased after her with Queen Marie's jewels. All she could do now for France's royal family was to keep them in her prayers, and hope that France's citizens forgave them of their crimes to their people.

It felt good to be back in her normal clothes, she thought, but she enjoyed wearing breeches. She kept them to wear for another day when she would need them. She completed her look with a pleated cotton mobcap with a ruffled brim. Hunger pains were talking to her. She tried to forget how she missed her long hair and made her way downstairs to order a big breakfast, and to question the couple that kept the tavern.

"Do you know of a friendly farmer who would help my brother and me with a ride to Mr. Thomas Jefferson's home?"

"Yes," answered the bone skinny tavern man. "The closest one is about five miles away. He owns his own dairy farm and has a pung that he drives to town frequently."

"What is a pung?"

"I can tell you just got off a ship with that thick French accent of yours," giggled the voluptuous tavern keeper's wife. A pung is a sleigh pulled by two horses."

"Oui, yes," exclaimed Angelina, "just off the *Victorious*. A pung is just the thing we need. "What is this farmer's name?"

"Mr. Kettler," the tavern keeper answered for his wife, "He is German farmer, north of here. Walk up Main Street for one mile, and it will be off to the left, four miles up the road. He will take you in for the night, I am sure."

"Tis, two weeks to Christmas," the tavern keeper's wife declared, "and a blizzard is a comin'.

I recommend you take some of your money, and get yourselves some warmer clothes. Your gonna need to bundle up before you head out of town."

"Thank you for your hospitality and advice." Angelina almost went into a curtsy out of habit, but she fought against it since there was no need to curtsy anymore. The art of the curtsy had always been a big deal in her world in France. It was still strange at times thinking of that life being gone forever now. Her world had been focused all on Princess Marie. It was awful, Angelina thought, that they didn't know each other anymore. She hoped and prayed that the royal family were safe and unharmed.

Jacque's job was out buying new things they needed in Norfolk such as new winter coats, gloves, boots, and blankets. She gave her wool blanket on the ship to Pierre, she didn't want a blanket that smelled after months of being in dirty water and body odors. Pierre needed it more, she thought, if he was going back to France in the winter weather.

Angelina's job was to find a gentleman who was traveling towards where the German farmer lived. With help again from the tavern keeper, she found a gentlemen who was travelling that way, so they didn't have to walk in the snow. Once the gentleman had finished his business within a couple of hours, they traveled over snow-covered hills.

"I will knock on the farmer's door to see if he's feeling hospitable," offered the gentleman, when they pulled onto his property.

"Who have you got with you?" asked the German farmer to the gentleman, as he walked out of his stone farmhouse to meet the newcomers.

"We have crossed the Atlantic from France to make a new life," Jacque answered for them.

"We need to get to Thomas Jefferson's Monticello home, for we are to be in his service," Angelina spoke out half-truths to him, when she climbed out of the pung. "We were told in town perhaps we could help you with what work needs attending to on your farm in exchange for a bed for the night and ride to Monticello."

"You two look like you could use a hot meal," remarked the farmer. "Surely, I will. My home is your home for the night. Go warm yourselves by the fire. My animals need to be fed later, the manure mucked, and the horses are going to need to have blankets on them before we lock the barn for the night."

Mr. Kettler's wife welcomed them at once with German walnut shortbread Christmas cookies and milk. The tantalizing aromas of beef and freshly baked bread filled the air, which smelled so wonderful that she could barely wait to eat.

Once the German farmer said grace by candlelight, Angelina and Jacque were served a wealthy man's meal from hot bowls filled with wonderful peppery beef stew, baked country loaf bread with sweet butter, and fresh cold glasses of milk. Angelina never thought that she would eat beef stew like the beef bourguigon in France again, she thought, but it was like France's beef stew. It was still delicious even with no French red wine, nor mushrooms. Only lots of salt and pepper with carrots, onion, and potatoes.

Everyone attended to the duties on the dairy farm after nightfall, Angelina had a full a night of complete enjoyment. Mrs. Kettler, a very friendly, very talkative English woman, told her many stories of her childhood in England, and more stories of England's farms of the wealthy that she had lived and worked on as tenants while they walked to the dairy. Mrs. Kettler talked on and on about all their cows, and had given her a recipe for a famous English cream cheese.

Afterwards, they all warmed up with hot chocolate and huge servings of chocolate buttermilk cake that had three layers to it with Mrs. Kettler's special chocolate cream cheese frosting on top and in between the layers. Cold Pumpkin pudding was served on the side. It was a blessing to eat such a rich cake. She loved the flavor and creaminess in the chocolate frosting from Mrs. Kettler's homemade cream cheese. Angelina had felt like celebrating since they had arrived safely in

America. Now with the chocolate cake and hot chocolate, she felt that it was a celebration. The pumpkin pudding was something new that was delicious. Spicy and sweet, she ate it all slowly to enjoy every bit of her dessert. She was determined to get all the recipes from dinner to dessert and the German walnut shortbread recipe from Mrs. Kettler. She succeeded, and had them all written down in her diary using her quill, ink, and powder.

By seven o'clock in the morning, Mr. Kettler hitched up the pung with the trunks packed. Mrs. Kettler brought out a basket of ham sandwiches and sealed jars of water for their trip. Blankets were flung over the trio to shield them from the freezing winds. The sky was chalky white for the threat of a blizzard lingered in the air.

"It is going to take most of the day," Mr. Kettler informed them, "to get to Monticello with the snow already coming down and the blizzard not far behind."

Traveling up the mountain, Angelina daydreamed of her past winters in France, comparing it to the mountainous beauty of Virginia that surrounded her. In her opinion, France had lost the wild natural beauty of the countryside. Angelina was enthusiastic as they headed north. The pung glided through miles of snow-covered woods overflowing with trees and rabbits. At times, they drove north through other prosperous settlements such as Williamsburg, Richmond and Charlottesville. Quickly, it grew very dark and the weather drastically changed. Snow fell in massive drifts with harsh icy winds.

The horses were doing their best to keep up, but the snow was getting too deep. After about six hours, Mr. Kettler started to lose the way.

"The horses can't go any farther," shouted Mr. Kettler, as the blizzard started blowing hard around them. "We're going to have to go back!"

"No," shouted Angelina, "we'll walk the rest of the way up there."

"It's only a mile up the mountain." Mr. Kettler informed them. "Are you sure?"

"Yes, we have to make it there tonight." They climbed out of the pung with their trunks before the farmer tried to stop them.

"Farewell to you," replied the German gentleman farmer. "Can't do long good-byes. You both better get going before you freeze to death." He turned the pung around and descended down the mountain. Angelina and Jacque waved good-bye and headed up the last remaining mile of the mountain to Monticello.

Luckily, the German farmer parted with them on the road that was the connecting road from the city of Charlottesville, to Monticello. They hiked on the road that led up to a cobblestone pathway towards the house that was surrounded by trees in the front yard.

"Jacques," said Angelina, when they walked up to the house, amazed at the sight of a simple red brink mansion. "It looks like a French chateau. What do you think?"

"It looks like an aristocrat's home."

They left their trunks at the bottom of a snow-covered earthen ramp that led up to the front door to the two-story red brick mansion, which had a bricked octagon shape around the front door located in the middle of the mansion. They walked quickly up to the front door and knocked.

Chapter 14

"Get off this property!" the young woman barked. "Go back to your homes!" The cruel girl slammed the front door shut.

"All hope is lost," Angelina exclaimed, as she looked at Jacque, panicked. "We are going to freeze to death. Where do we go? I can't see anything but snow."

A snow owl hooted in a tree above them. Angelina frantic, jumped into Jacque's arms from fright. Both their teeth chattered from the freezing cold blizzard. Angelina was truly terrified that she and Jacque could die that night. Her hopes of finding Thomas Jefferson were gone. She wanted to sit down and cry. She was tired and frustrated from being cold for so long since they left France. Now, she and Jacque were both going to die in the snow and no one would ever know.

"We will probably drop dead from the blizzard," cried Angelina dramatically, choking back tears of fear and misery.

"We have to build a shelter, Angelina. You can't give up hope. We are in the mountains. There are hundreds of trees. We have to use fallen branches to make a shelter to shield us overnight, or we will freeze to death! Leave our things here and we can build the shelter around our trunks. I didn't come all the way here from France just to die, and neither did you! We have to build a shelter before the sun goes down."

Angelina knew he was right. She didn't cross the ocean just to die on the snowy mountain top. Angelina gathered fallen limbs under the snow. Why had the girl who answered the door been so awful to them? Why had the girl been so cross with her when she asked if Mr. Jefferson was home? Had she lied to her? Was he in his home sleeping in his warm bed? She would never see her American friend again, she thought, if she could have only seen him. Then, everything would be as she planned it. If only, she could talk to Mr. Jefferson. He would know who she was. He wouldn't have sent her back out to catch her death out in the cold. Angelina grew angrier the longer she dwelled on the heartless young woman. Wasn't it Christmas time when people were supposed to be extra nice to others? This woman didn't care if she and Jacque froze to death. How could someone be so cruel in the middle of a blizzard of all things? This woman was evil to....

117

"AHHH! Jacque!" hollered Angelina! "I hurt my ankle. Where are you, Jacque? Can you hear me?"

"I'm here, Angelina!" he yelled, running to her. "What is wrong?"

"I sprained my ankle falling over a big tree branch. Can you help me up? She tried to stand up, but she flinched in pain and fell again. Jacque helped her up and used his strong arms to help brace her up. She limped over to sit on a tree stump with his help.

"I just know we are going to die!"

"You have to calm down!" Jacque bent down and glared at Angelina. She opened her mouth to yell that she would not calm down when she was stopped short. He put his finger to her lips. "Shhh," he ordered, as he stood up. "I think I hear something. I think the farmer came back for us."

"How can you hear anything?" she asked, as she sobbed.

"I see the lights of lanterns! I'm going to go check it out."

Angelina rubbed her sore ankle while she waited for Jacque to come back. She cried from the pain of her injury and the hopelessness of the situation. She prayed that Jacque could find her when he found someone, if he even saw anyone at all.

"Help-help!" Jacque shouted waving his arms running to a sleigh coming towards him, through the howling winds of the blizzard.

118

The driver stopped at once.

"Please Sir," Jacque bolted in front of the sleigh. "My friend and I are stranded on this mountain. My friend has sprained her ankle. "Could you please help us?"

"Of course, young man," announced the wealthy looking gentleman. He wore a white, high-neck shirt under a black blazer with buttons. His winter coat was sewn like his blazer, but long and made out of wool with metal buttons from top to bottom. "Where is your friend?"

"She is out this way, Sir," as Jacque pointed in the direction where he had come out of the woods.

The gentleman, the driver, and Jacque all headed out to find Angelina.

The gentleman was the first to spot a figure shivering with cold. Right away, his driver standing beside him, picked Angelina up, and carried her to his sleigh before Angelina could say a word to fight them off. She was shocked seeing two strangers bundled up who had saved her. Angelina was reassured when she saw that Jacque was with them. He said not a word, but put their trunks in the sleigh, jumped in, crossed his arms across his body, shoving his hands into his armpits to warm himself in the sleigh. She figured that the thank you and introductions could be well enough said later under this gentleman's roof. However, Angelina had no idea who these men were and

119

where they were going. Everyone was too cold to talk.

Angelina and Jacque looked at each other relieved that they were lucky to be saved by this gentleman's kindness. Angelina looked over at the mystery man who had saved their lives, but with the snow all around them, she couldn't see her hand in front of her. This man would undoubtedly know who Mr. Thomas Jefferson was. He may even be on good terms with him to help her make their introductions. As the sleigh turned, they arrived at this gentleman's home. Both of them quickly recognized the residence. Angelina and Jacque were back at Monticello. Angelina suddenly realized that she must be sitting in Mr. Jefferson's pung. Angelina had finally found him. Had he seen her? She didn't care that she was going to see that evil girl again. She hoped that she would see her again, and that mean teenage girl would be embarrassed by her bad behavior towards them. Angelina was thrilled and grateful that she was finally there with Thomas Jefferson after all the trouble she had gone through to be sitting with him.

Once inside Monticello, Mr. Jefferson ordered his Negro's to fetch his guests' warm blankets and brandy to warm them up in front of the fireplace.

"I thought you two might be able to tell me how you managed to get yourselves on my little mountain in this blizzard." Mr. Jefferson began to make his introduction once he saw all had been taken care of to make these strangers warm and comfortable. "You two are lucky I was out tonight, or you indeed would have frozen to death.

"Monsieur Jefferson," Angelina began, "I have come from France to see you. It is me, Angelina Savoy, from the Palace Versailles. You do remember me, don't you?"

"Angelina," said Mr. Jefferson, as he put his hand over this mouth in shocked silence. He remembered her as, 'the little Chef of France'.

"I could not forget you, little mademoiselle. Why did you leave Versailles?"

"Oh," cried Angelina, "Mr. Jefferson, Have you not heard, or read the news about France? Versailles was attacked and mobbed by the angry peasant women and men. The royal family was captured and taken as prisoners away to the Tuileries Palace in Paris. I escaped with my life."

She proceeded to tell him the story of leaving Versailles, her meeting Jacque, and her adventures in getting to America to find her Uncle Claude.

"I was hoping to find you, so I could work for you and stay during the winter until the spring, and finish my journey north."

"You are blessed to be alive through your dangerous journey. I have just the thing for you and your friend. You can work in my kitchen as a kitchen maid because I know how much you love being in a kitchen. You can learn from my Head Chef, James Hastings. Remember, I took him to France with me to learn to become a Chef in the French ways. He has done well to prepare all of France's meals." He took her hands, rubbing his hands in hers in order to warm her up. He continued speaking to her while checking that her vital signs were good. "Do you remember how I told you that I was going to bring back with me different kinds of vegetable seeds? Now, that you are here, you can help me plant them in the spring."

He turned to face the young man, "What is your name young man?"

"Jacque, Sir," he answered as he straightened up.

"Young man, you can work as one of my stable boys. You two will have a fine time here. I will help you two plan for your trip in the spring. By spring, there will be settlers wanting to travel north in wagon trains. I am confident that I will know of one when the snow starts to thaw. Until then, you are settled here."

"Thank you, Monsieur Jefferson," Angelina answered while she shivered, her teeth chattered, and her ankle throbbed. Angelina kissed his hand. "I am grateful that you rescued us."

"No need for that, girl. I am not royalty. We are friends. I am glad to help you and your friend.

"Let me show you where you will be sleeping." Mr. Jefferson rose and walked from the parlor through the entrance hall to the front of the house where there were two guest bedrooms on the north wing of Monticello. "Jacque, you will sleep in the north square room. Angelina, you will sleep in the next room, the north octagonal room. Tomorrow, I will have my daughter, Miss Martha, show you around and make the introductions to who will be your superiors.

"You two need a good night's sleep after all that you have been through this night."

In the privacy of her room, Angelina settled in a soft, warm bed. Her ankle still throbbed a little, but she couldn't complain because she was finally at Monticello. He even said, she reflected, that he wanted to help her with her journey. She listened to the hard winds and snow hitting the window panes. Two smells – the bite of wood smoke from the fireplace and of sweet lavender lingered on her skin from a proper washing up - twisted into a perfume that took her back to the Palace of Versailles. Lost in her thoughts, she wondered where Princess Marie was on a night like this. Was the princess freezing to death as she almost froze to death that night? She sat up in her bed, drank all the water from a pewter cup that had been given to her on the small table next to the bed. Fresh water, Angelina thought as she finished it, never tasted so good. She hobbled over to the window, sat down in a chair in the room, and watched the blizzard for a while.

The snow was coming down hard and she enjoyed watching the white wisps of snow. She prayed, "Thank you God," that she had made it. Silently, she cried tears of relief that she was alive and well after escaping out of France.

Chapter 15

The East Lawn - the front of the plantation house, sat on the top of a 850-foot high peak in the Southwest Mountains south of the Rivanna Gap. Mr. Thomas Jefferson named his home, 'Monticello' from the Italian word "Little Mountain." A large towering two-story red brick structure with four square shaped, stained wood pillars in the front of it. The second floor had a door that came out to a balcony that was attached to the four wood pillars that went from the top of the wooden awning roof to the bottom of the front porch. The façade on the first floor of the red brick mansion had ten windows. Each side had five windows on each side and each side end of the first floor had a small door. The upper level had six windows, three on each side and a side window on each end. Angelina stared at the front of Mr. Jefferson's home. She thought it looked like a Roman temple with the columns that she had seen in a book with the princess at her side. Angelina had woken up early to a clear, bright sunny morning to go for a walk and explore Mr.

Jefferson's property. She wanted to walk on her ankle a little to see if it still hurt, which surprisingly it only did a little. With eagerness and the expectation of a good day, she felt like something great was going to happen to her today. Her new life awakened her with the anticipation of a new chapter in her life. The property was so spectacular after the night's blizzard into a sunny, glittery snow-covered world.

Angelina inhaled the fresh, crisp air while walking back. She didn't want to go too far with her injured ankle, and risk hurting it again. Back in her room, she unstitched her wool coat to take the jewels out when she heard a knock on the door.

"Hello, is someone in there" the voice asked.

Angelina knew that voice and her belly cringed.

"Yes, Madame," she answered politely. "I am here."

"May I please come in?" The voice asked.

"Yes, Madame." And Angelina opened the door.

It was the young woman that answered the front door when they had first arrived, kicking them off the property. Angelina studied her when she opened the door. She was a well-dressed, tall and slim, teenage girl of seventeen. Her red hair was kept in a ruffled cap, and curls fashioned around her angular face. Following behind her, an African girl carried a ceramic basin and pitcher with steaming hot water in it. Angelina watched the girl set them down on the table next to the bed.

"I am Miss Martha," she introduced herself to Angelina, "I am Mr. Jefferson's daughter. Everyone calls me 'Miss Pasty'." She turned to the African girl. "This is Critta, she is one of our housemaids. You need to take off your dress and undergarments. Give me the ones you brought over from France. I don't know what kinds of germs you have brought here. Filthy things! I shall have Critta take them and give them to the slave men to burn. My father has said that I am to provide you with new dresses. There is a lump of bayberry soap in the basin and a washcloth. Wash your hair and body thoroughly.

"Critta will bring you fresh water to rinse off and rosewater. Use the rosewater after to rinse your face and your body, especially under your armpits. You will be provided with new petticoats and dresses for now that were mine, until better ones can be made. When you are finished, Critta will bring you to me. I will show you where you will be living and show you around the plantation."

Angelina was surprised that this girl had not apologized to her. How rude, she thought, this girl never even mentioned the fact that she shut the door in her face. She quickly cleaned up, rinsed off with the fresh water and rosewater that Critta brought to her. Angelina took her time while she changed into her undergarments and best mobcap trimmed with lace. Other days she could wear her plain mobcaps, she thought, but for today all she wanted to do was make a good first impression. There were cotton undergarments and six dresses that another negro girl had laid out on the bed. They all looked old fashioned compared to her fancy French dresses, Angelina thought, there is no way that I am going to let that mean girl burn my fine, French dresses.

One dress was white linen patterned with little red roses all over it. One dress was made of a solid light blue cotton and another cotton dress was white and pine tree green of vertical stripes. There was a dress that was made of pink linen that was patterned with little white flowers all over it. There was a cotton dress with red and white vertical stripes, and last was another cotton dress that had vertical stripes of royal blue and white. She was so thrilled when she saw new velvet black slippers. She changed into the white and red stripped dress because it looked festive for the Christmas season. Luckily, the slippers fit nice and tight, but she put her boots back on since they were going outside. She wished that she had a mirror to see herself in her first American dress.

Critta was a plain, quiet girl, leading Angelina through the house to Miss Martha's room without saying a word to her. It must be, she assumed that they weren't allowed to talk to the guests, or each other while they served the family. At least she was used to that since servants hadn't really talked to one another at Versailles either.

"It's a clean job and a good opportunity for you to learn to cook and see how an American plantation is lived on a daily basis working as a kitchen girl," Martha Jefferson declared in her snobbish tone, "so be grateful that my father took you in."

At that moment, a negro woman walked in.

"This woman is going to take your measurements, so she can make you some pinafores to go on top of your dresses. You don't want to get your dresses dirty when working in the kitchen."

When finished, Martha and Angelina walked out of the south square room, which was where Martha's office was in the back of the house on the first floor. Next, they entered the dining room.

"Breakfast is served at eight o'clock and dinner is served at four o'clock here in the dining room. Walking through the dining room, and into the next small room at the end of the house, takes you into the tea room. Tea is served later in here when my father requests. He usually drinks Imperial Tea."

Angelina noticed that Monticello was painted with whitewash inside each room. The entire house was in the process of being decorated to Mr. Jefferson's requests.

"The houseboy rings two bells. One rings an hour before the meal is served and the second when the meal is ready to be served.

"You will be expected to help prepare the meals, keep the coals hot on the stewstoves, and help keep the areas clean. The other kitchen help will work around you in the kitchen cutting, chopping, boiling, and roasting.

"Do you think you can remember all the instructions?"

"Yes, Madame."

"Bring your things out of the room you stayed in, put on your coat and boots. We are leaving the main house to where you will be living while you are working here for my father."

Angelina hoped that she was being led to the kitchen because she was getting hungry, but was led to a carriage. They stepped in while the negro driver loaded her trunk. Where is Jacque, she thought, I am sure that Mr. Jefferson is taking care of his lodging too. The driver drove on a long snow-covered dirt trail.

"This road is called 'Mulberry Row'," Miss Martha informed her. "It is the main plantation road that we use for many reasons."

They passed by many small wood cabins that were further down the plantation road that were built for Mr. Jefferson' workers. They stopped at a wood cabin. They stepped into the small housing unit with a fire place, two beds and a tall narrow wooden dresser with six drawers.

A dark-skinned girl, her hair parted in the middle with two thick corn rolled braids to the back of her head, walked into the cabin.

"Kiara," Miss Martha made the introductions, "this is the French girl that you will supervise. Make the introductions to James and show her the routine of the day. I will be down later to speak to James. I take my leave for church. I don't want to be late for the sermon. Angelina, mind you listen to Kiara, and everything will go smoothly."

"Yes, Madame." Angelina rolled her eyes as Miss Martha turned away, and left them.

Angelina noticed Kiara rolled her eyes too when Miss Martha walked out. She appeared mean, superior to Angelina. The two girls studied each other until Kiara spoke first.

"This bed is mine," Kiara said sarcastically. "That one is yours. It used to be my sister's, Critta, but we all had to change beds with you here."

"Sorry," replied Angelina, "I didn't know." She gazed over at her bed and was mesmerized by the multi-colored squares of a unique quilt. Angelina dropped her trunk that she lugged around next to her bed, and sat down on it. She gently touched the quilt's puffed-up squares of different material stitched together. It looked worn and the colors were faded. It looked like, she thought, a masterpiece of stitchery.

"It's a quilt my mother made by hand," said Kiara. "You will meet her soon enough. The bottom drawers are yours, and you have a hook for hanging your coat on the door", as she pointed to the door. "I don't care where you put your snow boots. Just don't put them on my side of the room. I don't want to step in a puddle."

"I don't want to step in a puddle either," replied Angelina. This girl made her feel like she was a child, she thought, even though they appeared to be the same age. She felt intimidated by her tone and bossiness. Angelina wondered how old this girl could be with being so self-confident. She always seemed to doubt her opinions and actions.

"Well, Miss Thing," started Kiara, "let's get moving to the kitchen. "I will introduce you to James, and then I will show you what's what."

"I have met your brother before, mademoiselle. When he was at the Palace of Versailles with Mr. Jefferson last summer. It will be nice to see him again."

"Oh, so you think you're all high and mighty since you lived in a palace. You think you're too good to work with us slaves with your fancy French accent and all."

"No," replied Angelina, politely not wanting to get on her bad side, "I was not royalty. I was a servant in Versailles."

"We'll see how fancy you are when you have to kill a pig for a fancy ham dinner."

Angelina rolled her eyes, and walked behind her as they left. She was filled with anger and confusion as to why this African girl had such hostility towards her. Angelina was not unlike her in that they both served masters. She had served a king's daughter. She had been at the princess' beck and call, day and night her whole life until now. Who was this girl to judge her? The more she thought of Kiara's uneducated opinions of her, the more it enraged her.

"Bonjour, Angelina," greeted James Hemming's. He gave her a warm hug, and Kiara left them. "Mr. Jefferson came to see me earlier to inform me you have come here from France. You will have to tell me all about how you came to be here. Only fate could bring us back together again."

"It is so good to see you again, James. You look like you are doing well. Have you placed France on the plates of Mr. Jefferson's friends? This kitchen is huge! It is so amazing with an entire wall of stewstoves. I love the fireplace! I will never be cold in here. Wow, look at that tall clock! I will tell you all that has happened with the royal family, and how I came to cross the Atlantic in private, between old friends. I have also brought a friend here with me too. Did Mr. Jefferson speak of Jacque to you?"

"As to your first question," answered James, laughing at her enthusiasm. "Yes, these rich colonials are saying my food is half-Virginian and half-French. The clock is so we are punctual on time for Mr. Jefferson's meals. Mr. Jefferson has not introduced me to Jacque, but I have heard of him here. I hear he is to work under Paul, the horseman in the stables."

"James, that is a beautiful compliment on your cooking. When do you think I could find Jacque later without angering your sister?"

"Oh, Kiara," he chuckled, "don't worry about her. You can try to find Jacque this evening after Mr. Jefferson has his pot of tea, usually around six o'clock. For now, Mr. Jefferson has instructed me to have you help me and send it all off to Kiara to serve. Are you hungry? I could make you eggs and toast quick."

"Yes, I would love that! Thank you!"

In the meantime, while they ate their breakfasts, Angelina spoke of Versailles to James about how she had to leave France. She spoke of Paris, Jacque, sailing on the ship, and landing in Norfolk. "What is it like here at Christmas time?

"This is my busiest time with the Christmas and New Year's parties the Master hosts. We are going to have long days of prepping, baking, roasting, cooking, and presentin' meals."

"I have brought my diary, she said excitedly, "to write all the meals. I will watch you prepare and write notes on how you do things in the kitchen."

"I had to write down all French recipes too when I learned from Monsieur Combeaux. He was the French caterer who provided the meals in Mr. Jefferson's Paris kitchen. You never learned how to cook at Versailles?"

"No, I just watched the Head Chef."

"Let's start rolling up them sleeves, and get cleanin' some sweet potatoes."

Over the fortnight, Angelina still hadn't looked for Jacque. She had been exhausted by the end of each workday since they arrived. All she had the energy for at the end of the day was to build the fire for another cold winter night and watch the snow fall on moonlit nights until she went to bed.

Time had flown by since she had started working. Angelina could hardly contain her excitement. Christmas was tomorrow.

Monticello was in full swing on Christmas Eve of decorating, cooking and entertaining for Thomas Jefferson's family and friends.

Angelina had been asked to come out of the kitchen to the main floor to polish the silver in the dining room. Presently, she was cleaning the elegant silver goblets that were Mr. Jefferson's favorites. Mr. Jefferson had them made when he had lived in Paris as the American ambassador, Trade Minister to France.

Angelina reflected on the past joyful festive holidays that she had shared and dined with France's royal family. At times, she still couldn't believe that she was here in America with Mr. Thomas Jefferson in his home. She would have loved to hear Christmas music like she had back in Versailles. Versailles had had its own Royal Chapel with musicians. Angelina sighed sadly, wondering what had happened to the royal family that she had loved so dearly. She distracted her downhearted thoughts away while she polished the goblets humming Christmas music until she could see her reflection in them. Once her job was completed, she walked back to the kitchen to continue to help James.

Kiara rushed in. "Mr. Jefferson wants to see you, Angelina, right away in Miss Martha's room, the south square room."

Angelina washed up from doing small tasks for James, hurried up to the main floor, and knocked on the open door. Martha was sitting down with her sewing, without looking up at her. Mr. Jefferson was aimlessly pacing the room.

"You called me, Monsieur Jefferson?"

"Did you polish the silver goblets in the dining room, Angelina?"

"Oui," she answered, "yes, Monsieur."

"Did you remove the goblets from the table and put them somewhere else?"

"No. I left them on the table."

"Liar," Martha proclaimed, with venom in her voice.

Martha's attack shocked Angelina. She could not believe that she was being accused and attacked by this evil girl.

"Monsieur Jefferson, I would never steal from you!"

"Father! She arrived like a thief in the night and now here before you is your proof. Kiara came to me to ask where the goblets were. This thieving little French girl was the last one to have her hands on them."

Angelina was horrified. She had only stolen once in her life, and she still suffered terrible guilt over stealing the jewelry from her queen. Angelina could barely stand. She felt her knees would collapse under her. What if Mr. Jefferson believed Miss Martha? Where would she go? What if Jacque stayed and she never saw him again? How could she tell the truth if the silver goblets were not found? She would be kicked out of Monticello into the winter cold and catch her death.

"I didn't steal them!" implored Angelina.

Angelina was dismissed back to the kitchen. Kiara was ordered to search their bedroom. James was ordered to comb through the kitchen.

The remainder of Christmas Eve, James was quiet and stayed away from Angelina.

She shoveled more hot small wood chunks burnt down and ash from the hearth with the little shovel that had a long handle, which was added to the coals to the hot stewstoves.

When Angelina got back to the cabin, she had brought firewood in to heat up the little house. Kiara wouldn't even acknowledge her as she started the fireplace. Angelina slept that night with bitterness in her heart for the fact that she had done nothing wrong.

Chapter 16

Christmas in the kitchen was hectic as the Africans moved around each other preparing the Christmas day meals. James and Kiara were avoiding her. Not one person acknowledged her. Christmas was supposed to be the happiest time of year, but she felt no one wanted her there.

Her plan for the day was to find the silver goblets, find out who stole them and inform Mr. Jefferson the truth about who stole them.

Mr. Jefferson and his family were going to Mr. and Mrs. John Adam's home later in the day, so she would be able to search Monticello after they left. Hopefully, she thought, she would find them, so Mr. Jefferson would have a wonderful night using them to drink her wine that she had brought with her from France.

Angelina was deep in thought over who wanted her out of Monticello. Kiara came to her mind because she was the one to tell Miss Martha that she was the last one to have the goblets. Martha was the second person she blamed. In Angelina's eyes,

Miss Martha was more passionate about her being there. Despising her for no reason, and making her life miserable at Monticello. It could be Critta. She had taken her bed, so why would Critta want her to stay.

At midday, once the Jefferson family left, she frantically searched the house. Angelina searched in secret the dining room, the tea room, and the kitchen pantry for the goblets. She was searching the dumbwaiter, which was the lift inside of the wall of the dining room, until Kiara snuck up behind her.

"What are you doing, 'Miss Thing'? Are you getting the goblets from out their hiding place? I knew you stole them. Couldn't stand it that you didn't have beautiful things anymore, so you had to take something for yourself before you left?"

"I didn't steal them," Angelina fire back. "I am trying to find them, and I will tell Mr. Jefferson the truth."

Angelina turned, and got up in Kiara's face. "Did you steal the goblets?"

"I have no reason to steal Mr. Jefferson's cups."

"Help me find them and find out who did."

Kiara's face softened. "So you didn't steal them?

"No, I told you that I didn't steal them. I am sorry," and Angelina backed away. "I don't mean to get mean. Please help me find them. I think I should check Miss Martha's room."

Both of the girls snuck to Martha Jefferson's room.

"Kiara, can you stay outside the door and make sure no one catches me in here while I check her room?"

"Yes, but make it quick before any of my kin come lookin' for me."

Angelina walked around, searched under Martha's bed, and searched around for any other hiding places that would be big enough to conceal them. She noticed Martha's small work table had a drawer. She hurried over to it, and opened the drawer. Nothing. Her heart jumped, she spotted a little wooden stick shaped like a wooden nail in the back, inside of the drawer. Pushing down on the left side of the wood stick, it sprang up from its position. A secret compartment in the drawer popped open. Angelina found them! She snatched the goblets out of the secret compartment, closed the latch to shut the secret compartment, closed the drawer, and rushed out to Kiara.

At midday on her break from the kitchen, she managed to sneak out, and ran down Mulberry Row, to her little wood cabin to grab a bottle of her French wine for Mr. Jefferson as a Christmas present. Angelina got back without James asking her where she went. She acted like she never left, and kept herself busy helping in the kitchen. Even though James was still giving her the cold shoulder, she put on her bravest face while she finished warming baguettes in the bake oven. Most of the day, she worked at her baking skills helping the baker by proofing yeast before adding the foamy yeast water into the flour mixture, kneading the bread dough, and waited for the bell to ring for when Mr. Jefferson arrived.

As the carriage pulled up to Monticello, Kiara rang the bell for all to be ready. Angelina was ready as well with her new found friend's help. Angelina was fed up with this cruel girl and Mr. Jefferson was going to know the truth. Finishing her work with the bread dough for now, she set the bread dough to rise by setting it aside covered with a dry towel warmed by the hearth fire to help the dough rise in a large ceramic bowl greased with butter.

Coming out of the Christmas carriage, Miss Martha still badgered her father before anyone heard them conversing in private.

"Father, when are you going to rid us of that little French thief?" Martha nagged him. "I am sure Christmas will not be the same with her around. What will she steal from us next? She is not fit to work here."

"Most likely, they have been misplaced. You will see Martha, the goblets will be found."

"Misplaced," Martha snapped on him, "Father, you certainly cannot mean that. You don't just

142

misplace two of the finest silver cups ever made. No, she has stolen them. I am sure."

Mr. Jefferson rolled his eyes and rang the dinner bell, as they stepped into the dining room.

"That girl is," replied Miss Martha as they sat down, "a troublemaker. I wish her charms didn't blind you so."

Mr. Jefferson patted her hand that rested on the dining room table nearest to him, "Martha, you have no proof that she stole my goblets, so please let us sit and enjoy our Christmas dinner."

Just then, James came out with their turkey, another worker came out with mashed potatoes and gravy, another followed with cornbread dressing, and others followed with trays of other sweet delicacies. Mr. Jefferson was overjoyed as Kiara set in front of him and Martha the two silver goblets. Then, she poured Angelina's wine in them to celebrate Christmas dinner.

"Miss Kiara, wherever did you find my goblets?" inquired Mr. Jefferson.

"I didn't, Mr. Jefferson. Angelina did while you were out earlier today on your holiday visits."

"Could you please call her in?"

"Yes, Mr. Jefferson." Kiara put the bottle on the table in front of him to admire the bottle, but not before she saw Miss Martha squirm in her chair.

Angelina strolled into the dining room anxious to clear her good name.

"Where did you find my goblets, mademoiselle?"

"I found them in Miss Martha's room, in her working table drawer. I personally gave Kiara the French wine that I brought over for you to have a bottle as my Christmas present to you for letting Jacque and me stay here.

"Thank you, Angelina." He drank from his goblet. "It is wonderful." Mr. Jefferson turned to his conniving daughter. "Martha!" He shouted, so the entire house heard. "Would you care to explain how she found the goblets in your room."

"Father," whimpered Martha, "I thought you would throw her out as a thief with no regret. I'm sorry, but you pay more attention to this girl than me."

"Martha! You should be ashamed for what you did! Your actions are of a spoiled girl. This girl deserves all the Christian charity we can give her! She had to escape from her home! How could you be so cruel to my guest? She is to stay here only until the spring. You need to apologize to Angelina. Not me!"

"I am sorry," Angelina," said Miss Martha red-faced, softly. "My actions were out of jealousy. I am truly sorry."

"I forgive you, Miss Martha." Angelina would forgive, but she would never forget how awful this girl was. She would never trust her, and would always be on her guard around this evil girl until she left for good. She would never let Mr. Jefferson know her true feelings towards his daughter, she thought, out of respect for him.

Christmas day was the longest day Angelina had ever worked. By the end of the day, her body ached terribly from head to toe. She still loved working in the kitchen. It was exciting in there, but she didn't realize how tiring it could be as well.

For her own Christmas present to herself, she had taken the time to build a roaring fire in her cabin, and boiled water and snow in a large cast-iron bowl that had three tall legs on to it made of the same cast-iron, so that you could have enough space underneath to make a little fire for boiling. She brought with her to wash up, a lavender soap bar from a set of five scented soap bars that Mr. Jefferson had given her for Christmas. Her big Christmas present from Thomas Jefferson, which he had gifted her was a grown up sized pale purple silk dress with two purple ribbons for her hair and a pair of velvet black shoes to go with it. He had it specifically made for her for when she turned sixteen. She had been so touched when she received it, she thought, how she had given him a hug and a kiss on the check. Afterwards, she had gotten suddenly embarrassed at herself over her silly behavior, but she had been overwhelmed by his kindness.

Relaxed, and smelling like lavender flowers after a proper washing up, Angelina soaked her overworked feet. She closed her eyes and reflected on the past Christmas's with Princess Marie. Was the royal family able to be together for Christmas? Did they get to celebrate Christmas this year?

Far in the distance, Angelina heard the echoes of lively music with drums and singing. She dried her feet, walked over to her tapestry bag, and pulled out a light blue silk dress with a lace square neckline that she brought with her from France. Miss Martha had not taken all of her dresses. She kept some hidden in her tapestry bag and her leather bag that had been packed in her trunk. It was a warm night with no snow falling or heavy breezes. She put on her cotton undergarments, mobcap, wool cloak, and boots. Angelina ventured out into the moonlit night to find out where the music was coming from. She was so excited that she wanted to run, but didn't risk ruining her special dress.

The moonlight on the snow lit up the night. When Angelina got closer, she smelled the smoke of wood burning, roasting meat and listened to laughter floating in the air. Angelina's eyes adjusted to the bright glow of a fire pit and glanced over the little groups of silhouettes of people around the fire keeping themselves warm.

"Awwww!" She screamed, so loud that others looked her way, and turned to look behind her. "You scared me, James."

"What are you sneaking around for?   You are welcome to join us."

"I didn't want to disturb you," said Angelina blushing. "I just heard the music, and I wanted to see where it was coming from."

"It is my family and friends having our own Christmas party. You don't have to be afraid."

A wide smile spread across her face. "I am not afraid. I didn't think you wanted to speak to me."

"I know," replied James, "I have acted awful, and I'm sorry. Come and meet my mother. We have the leftover turkey. We have all the leftovers and some specialties of our own. Don't you know all the real good parties start after the sun goes down?"

Angelina laughed. She was led to the gathering, and introduced to the grand lady mom of the Hemmings, Elizabeth Hemmings.

"Everyone calls me 'Miss Betty', announced the grand lady.

Late in the night, walking around the circle of the firepit warming up, she thought of Jacque. Would she be able to find him tonight?

She sang Christmas carols and danced some jigs with James around the gigantic fire pit. All the Africans were there. The older men sat on wooden stumps.   The older women huddled together around the food to make sure everyone got fed. Men, women, boys, and girls danced together and talked in their little groups.

Finally, she and Jacque had found each other at the fire pit. Her heart thrilled as he told his stories of how he liked Monticello, what he was doing in his work life, and where he was staying.

"My job is cold at times in the stables working with the horses, but it feels good working with my hands like the other boys. I have to answer to an older African boy, Paul. He is a nice fellow."

The night was the most fun of her life in America with food, dancing a few jigs and reels under the moon with Jacque, getting to know the other worker girls, and Kiara and her becoming friends.

Jacque walked her back to her cabin, so he would know where she was when he could get away. They saw each other in another light that night under the Christmas stars. The magic of a moonlit night stirred something new in them, and they only wanted to enjoy each other's company.

Chapter 17

Early April rainstorms flooded Monticello. All around the fields and footpaths, the soil smelled sweet like fresh, clean spring water that emerges when the forest floor and warms and arises up from the earth. Boots were caked with sticky mud, making walking harder. One and all on the plantation longed for days of warm, bright sunshine.

Mr. Jefferson took it upon himself as his responsibility to help Angelina and Jacque.

In Angelina's free time, she studied maps and read books that Mr. Jefferson thought she should learn from. She also learned American history from him in his library in the late afternoons. She had missed her school time with the princess. Angelina thought how much she missed and enjoyed reading. It was so exciting when she stared at the map of the United States, looking down on the Northwest Territory. Her heart jumped when Mr. Jefferson pointed out on a map to her the great lakes with Mackinac Island drawn on it from a large book that contained a collection of large maps.

It is such a long way to go. I wonder how long it will take us to get there?

Mr. Jefferson went into the city, Charlottesville, once a week to the Charlottesville Courthouse, which was where city business was done. He would find out at the courthouse where and when the summer wagons were heading out of Virginia. Angelina and Jacque waited eagerly down in the kitchen for Mr. Jefferson to return, yet no word.

Unexpectedly, Mr. Jefferson called for Angelina and Jacque during his tea time.

"One wagon train is due to head north at the end of April. Their first destination is to stop halfway through the journey at a permanent settlement in the northern territory, northeast of the Ohio River. The town is named, 'Marietta'. Angelina learned that an Ohio Company of Associates built this settlement in the Northwest Territory in 1788. The company's investors renamed it Marietta from originally being named Adelphia, meaning 'brotherhood' after Queen Marie Antoinette, in honor of France's contributions to the American victory in the American Revolution." Angelina wished that Queen Marie knew how the Americans loved her.

On the final leg of the journey, Angelina and Jacque had been informed by Mr. Jefferson that he learned from the Charlottesville city's settlers that colonials traveled on ships from Great Lake Erie up to Great Lake Huron to reach Mackinac Island.

Mr. Jefferson sold most of the remaining jewels to his friends' wives, Abigail Adams, Martha Washington, and Dolley Madison for a high price. Angelina used some of the money to pay Mr. Jefferson for the provisions that he helped provide for the journey. She still had plenty of money to use to settle down with once she got to the Mackinac Island, and she kept a few rings, earrings, and necklaces for herself to wear when she grew up. They would be cherished by Angelina to wear in memory of the loving mother that Queen Marie had been to her. Queen Marie would have loved to know that I wear all of her jewels, she thought, instead of the vile French women who hated her. She sewed the currency into the lining of her wool coat that would keep her warm. Angelina was wealthy enough to live comfortably for two lifetimes.

In exchange for helping Angelina find buyers for the jewelry, having Mr. Jefferson's slaves build their wagon, helping pack the wagon with food and supplies, and helping find the wagon train travelling up into the Northwest Territory, Angelina's job was to write detailed letters to him on every aspect of their journey. He wanted letters to tell him where they were, what they saw each day, names of people who they met, what they did, how far they traveled each day, and when they arrived in Ohio and Mackinac Island.

"Writing to me will be your job to inform me of the land whether it is mountainous country or, grassy plains. Write me of the lakes, rivers, and oceans. Write to me of the Native Americans. Write to me of what Nation they are. Draw me what they look like. I have a box of colored pencils for you," he said as he grabbed a small rectangle shaped wooden box off his desk, and handed it to her. "This is for you to draw me the colors of the Native Americans. Draw their clothes. Use the colored pencils to show me the colors of their clothes. You can draw me the colors of mountains, the land, and colors of lakes, rivers, and other bodies of water. Whatever you feel that you think is worth knowing. Write to me details of the woods you pass through. Write to me of conversations you have with settlers, and if you meet a Native American. Draw me animals that you see all the way on your journey.

"The Northwest Territory is wild, untamed land that needs to be explored and needs to be further discovered. Our new president, George Washington, will be eager to read your letters of your travels that I show him."

Angelina and Jacque set out at the end of April 1790, with heavy hearts and heartfelt goodbyes. Angelina and Kiara hugged as sisters. Kiara rolled her eyes at herself for showing such tender affections. Angelina promised to write to her. James Hemmings whispered to her that he should have gone with her while they embraced in a farewell hug. Angelina looked over at Jacque while he was saying his good-byes to his friends and shaking Paul's hand. Mr. Jefferson and Martha bid their farewells. Angelina vowed to keep Mr. Jefferson and America's new president, George Washington on her new mission.

They started late since it had rained the night before, the ground would be too muddy if they had left early in the day. Angelina and Jacque rolled out, and left Monticello forever in a new wood covered wagon. It had wooden hickory bows to hold the canvas top up. The canvas was smooth as silk to the touch because it had been rubbed with whale oil to keep the rain from coming in.

Inside, the middle of the wagon was made into a bed with a mattress, so it was a normal bed size. Everything was packed around the bed. The wagon was fully stocked with their trunks, a mason jar of coffee beans with coffee grinder, salt pork, rolls of sausages, dried corn, dried beans, dried apples, dried onions, flour, sugar, sweet butter, iron skillet and kettle, blankets, pillows, furs, a musket, bullets, axe, the colored pencil box, and a new writing box with parchment ready to record the daily adventures that were yet to be on the trail north. The wagon was led by oxen to cross over mountain ranges, grassy plains, and enormous hilltops.

They arrived at the starting point in the city, Charlottesville, which was where the other wagons were gathering at the courthouse. It was to be led by experienced men who had fought in the American Revolution, and admired Frontiersmen who were respected by Nations of Native Americans that spoke their languages.

Secretly, Angelina was in fear of this part of the journey traveling with strangers and led by strangers. Having never met them, would they be cruel men? What made them so experienced? Were they to be trusted? Have they ever killed any Native Americans? How many Native Americans had they killed? Were they friends with all Native American tribes? Angelina had so many unanswered questions. She wanted to question the wagon leaders, yet she was afraid to speak her mind. What if they didn't want to speak with her because she was a girl?

Over the next few weeks, twelve wagons were getting acquainted with each other and getting familiar with the wilderness that surrounded them. They passed sprouting fresh greenery on the forest floor, tender leaves on the hundreds of trees, and wildflowers budding over clear blue, sunny skies.

At night, in the comfortable bed of their wagon, Angelina pulled out the writing box, and wrote her first letter to Mr. Thomas Jefferson of her first days on the trail. She drew using the colored pencils, patches and fields of new and rare, striking blue, little red, bright orange, yellow and white wildflowers she saw. After that she wrote Kiara her first letter. Later in her diary, she wrote that she wished she knew where Princess Marie was, so she could write her a letter while Jacque slept from hard days of driving the wagon. She didn't think it was awkward for them to be sleeping together in the bed. They didn't see each other naked. She started thinking more and more of Jacque with loving affections.

She had turned fourteen over the winter, yet she felt older for all that they had been through together. He may fall in love, she thought, with some girl from Mackinac when they got there. He was a man in her eyes, so he would have to tell her how he felt first. In her opinion, love could ruin a friendship if one person doesn't love the other.

Crossing overland, Angelina still had worries of getting to know strangers in this new country. However, Angelina nodded in acknowledging a young bride a year or two older than her and started making friends with her. This girl looked friendly enough, she thought. Three weeks in the journey to Ohio, Angelina noticed her going into another's wagon. The young bride didn't notice that Angelina had seen her when she pulled out a bowl full of flour. Angelina saw her put a cloth over the bowl to keep it in, so the wind wouldn't catch it. Angelina hid, watched her smile when she walked away from the wagon. Angelina didn't like her sneaky behavior. It seemed to her, she thought, no one goes into another's wagon. Yet, she didn't know if that was something that the people that owned the wagon let her do. Maybe, they had an arrangement. It was really none of her business. Angelina decided that it would be a good idea to keep an eye on this thief. Angelina didn't want to confront her, she hated confrontation. She would introduce herself first, she decided, and after she had made friends with the thieving bride, she would find out her true colors. Angelina didn't want to accuse her, stirring up trouble. She still lacked confidence speaking out being a servant her whole life.

In the meantime, she traveled through the ups and downs of the countryside with fear of the Natives attacking the wagon party by surprise coming out of the wooded trails.

Occasionally, other families mentioned items missing. Angelina knew who was to blame, but she had no proof as of yet. Every family in the wagon train at times was asked to give up some of their flour, salt pork, or sugar for meals since they ate together for breakfast and supper. This bothered Angelina and Jacque since they didn't have much food to give away. They agreed that they felt they were being taken advantage of. They wanted to appear friendly and agreeable, so they kept quiet about it. Eventually, Angelina made friends with the possible thief and young bride, Helen Thomas, over a group supper and made small talk sitting by the bonfire. Angelina discovered that Helen knew a lot about farming and growing things. Helen knew about wild berries and other plants that grew in the wild, good and bad, such as wild onions, carrots, and cherries. She taught Angelina about the poisonous plant that could kill you if you ate it that looked like a carrot, called water hemlock.

One late spring afternoon, Angelina and Helen went out picking wild cherries where they were seen close by where they stopped to camp. Jacque came along with his musket to hunt and to use for protection out in the wilderness. Angelina and Helen had agreed to separate, so as not to get in each other's area for the picking. Jacque had left to hide in the trees thinking that it would be easier to see any animals, or threats from above the treetops. Angelina peacefully picked cherries, when she heard footsteps behind her, softly treading on the ground. Angelina turned around. A Native American man sprang up behind her. She screamed and dropped her basket. The Indian

157

grabbed her. Jacque jumped down from the tree to rescue her while Angelina was fighting against being caught as a hostage, or worse. Jacque shot his gun at the Native in an attempt to kill him, Jacque missed. The Indian realized that Jacque had tried to kill him, and pushed Angelina to the ground. Angelina terrified, watched the Native run at Jacque hitting him with the back of his hand hard, knocking him to the ground. Angelina watched in horror as Jacque was being strangled to death. On the Indian's right hip from behind his back, she saw his knife. Rage consumed her. No one was going to take her love away from her. She rushed towards the Indian from behind, snatched the knife. She stabbed the Native American with one hard thrust through the back of his neck and killed him. He fell immediately on his side to the ground, gurgling on his blood.

"Oh my God," said Jacque astonished, "you killed him! Are you OK? We have to bury him, "so, no one knows what we've done."

He rubbed his hands on his throat to soothe the pain, and was panting hard from the fight.

"I am fine, but what about Helen? She is bound to come any moment now after hearing the gunshot."

"You go look for her. I will bury the Native. We don't want anyone knowing what happened. We don't know what could happen to us."

"Did you get any blood on you?" asked Angelina.

"Yes, some. Did you?"

"No! Jacque, it wouldn't be wise to come back to the wagon until you shoot a rabbit. or a deer, or people will ask questions."

"Oui, to be sure. I will stay out all night if I have too."

"No. Just be careful. I don't want any more Natives finding you either."

And Angelina ran off looking for Helen. Suddenly, it came to her what to do.

"Helen! Helen!" She screamed.

"I am here," Helen answered, running into the clearing where Angelina was. "I heard the gunshot. What happened?"

"Jacque tried killing a deer, and he went after it. Let's get back. I have to start supper before Jacque gets back."

Chapter 18

A ngelina and Jacque traveled on not talking about what had transpired with the Native American man. Crossing the Ohio River was the biggest worry in the wagon party, and they were not looking forward to it.

The leader of the wagon party, Henri was a great surprise to Angelina. He was a big French middle-aged man with black hair who had come over to America when he was a young man to become a fur trapper, but he had gotten sucked in to help fight in the American Revolution like her father had. Late at night, Henri, Angelina and Jacque frequently spoke around the bonfire in their native tongue. Henri respected Angelina. He looked after her as a father would a daughter. He liked Jacque too. He admired him as a mature young man with a good head on his shoulders. Often at nights Henri found comfort in their long talks about France and when he was a young garcon.

A week after killing the Native American man, Angelina and Jacque stressed over whether any strangers would come out of the wilderness looking to find the missing Native man. One night, the cold sent the families to bed earlier. Jacque went off to sleep after having his share of the conversation with Henri. In low whispers, Angelina confessed to him what had happened with the Native American.

Henri looked straight into her eyes, with the most serious expression.

"What did he look like?"

"The Indian had a haircut that scared me. He had both sides of his head shaved except for the hair that went straight down the middle of his head. It was black, and the front of his hair stood up straight off his head. The back of his hair was long. Also, he had a hoop earring with a pendant. His face was hard, scars on his cheeks, and tan."

"What was he wearing?"

"No shirt," she blushed thinking about her first time seeing an Indian man with no shirt on. He had lots of muscles in his arms. He was strong. He wore breeches, but not out of material that we use, or from what I am accustomed to seeing. I don't know what they were made of."

"Sounds like a Shawnee warrior to me. The breeches are made out of deerskin," he laughed as he watched her face turn and pinch up when he told her about using deer hides to make breeches. "Ever since the Treaty of Fort Harmar in December of '88', the Shawnee have attacked more white settlers than ever."

"That is gross using deer skin for breeches! What is the Treaty of Harmar?"

"It was a meeting that the Northwest Territory's Governor Arthur St. Clair held at Fort Harmar. The fort is near to Marietta, where we are headed. Governor St. Clair invited all the Indian Chiefs to negotiate an agreement to stop the Indian threats. The idea for the meeting was to make peace because the United States government didn't have the currency to supply the US Army with weapons to handle the Indians threatening the white settlers.

"A friend of mine, Henry Knox, is the Secretary of War. He told me that he demanded the Governor have this meeting, so settlers could go on in peace after all the killing of Indians and whites over the land they wanted. All the Indian representatives went to Fort Harmar, from the Wyandot tribe, the Delaware tribe, the Ottawa tribe, the Potawatomi tribe, the Chippewa tribe, and the Sauk tribe.

"In the end, the Treaty didn't do anything to stop the bloodshed between the settlers and the Native Americans. Most of the Nations of Indians refused to honor the Treaty, along with the Shawnee Indians. The Shawnees argued that the other Indian Nations represented at the Treaty talks did not speak for them.

"The man you described to me sounds to me like a Shawnee warrior. He either would have killed you on the spot, or taken you back to his people as

162

a trophy, and eventually made you his wife. What did you do with the body?"

"Jacque buried it while I came back with Helen."

"Does she know?"

"No, she doesn't even know that we were attacked. Do you think the Shawnee are watching us in this place?"

"No, or else, I think we would have been attacked by now. All I can say for now is that we have to make sure to have our muskets ready, and get to Marietta as quick as we can."

"How far are we from Marietta, Ohio?"

"Not much further. As soon as we cross the Ohio River though, I feel we will be safe."

Angelina didn't get much sleep while she slept with the loaded musket, and waited half asleep if something would happen. More awake than ever the next morning, she drove the wagon and let Jacque sleep in. She drove on quietly waiting for the sounds or, voices of Native Indians, if an attack should arise. She felt better knowing that she had their musket underneath the box seat. When Jacque woke, she retold the story to Jacque from the night before of the confession she made to Henri. Angelina told him what Henri had told her of the Fort Harmar Treaty and the Shawnee warrior.

"I'm relieved that you did tell him what happened. I was thinking that he could help us find out if more Natives are hiding out in these woods. I thought maybe Henri could speak their language, or do something useful if we do get attacked?"

"He never mentioned speaking any Indian languages. I don't know if he does or not. All Henri said was that we need to cross the Ohio River as soon as we can to get out of harm's way."

Crossing the Ohio River was terrifying to Angelina when she saw it. It was the most significant body of water she had seen since the Atlantic. She was even more scared than she was before when she crossed the Atlantic because they were to cross the Ohio River in little rickety wooden flatboats that the men were to build at their campsite.

All day and night, the men cut down trees and used rope to make flatboats to carry them across the river. Long sticks were carved that would be used to push the flatboats from the bottom of the river, and to push the raft in the direction they wanted to go. Other men made oars to use in the deep water.

Angelina helped the women cook salted pork, baked beans with cornbread, and prepare camp for the long night to come of helping prepare for the river crossing. As everyone retired for the evening, Angelina walked to Helen's wagon. Walking towards her wagon, she heard someone inside the wagon scrambling about with a lantern still on, so she thought she would pay a visit before she called it a night. She climbed up and opened the wagon flap to investigate.

"Good evening, Helen."

Helen sprung up in front of her and shut the flap with a swipe of her hand in Angelina's face, but not before Angelina got a good glimpse of what was inside her cabin. Furniture up to the side of the wagon top, china plates scattered on top of her bed, and little pretty tea spoons, and other scattered pieces of clothing.

"Are you all right?" asked Angelina.

"Yes, I am fine. Sorry, but I am tired, and I am just getting ready for bed, I'm not decent."

Angelina didn't want to arouse Helen's suspicions of what Angelina already saw and knew.

"All right, I will see you in the morning."

She knew she had found the thief. All through the camp, the ladies had complained of losing something they cherished such as one of their china plates. The ladies assumed that one of their children had accidentally broken it while washing it and lied about it. The missing fancy silver tea spoons, a shawl, or a petticoat now and then. Now, she had her evidence. Should she notify Henri, or the ladies missing their silly things. Should she let it go? On the one hand, she wanted to tell on her. On the other hand, Angelina felt sorry for her. Why did Helen think that she needed to steal? She went to bed feeling at war with herself over what she should do.

At sunrise, she woke early to make biscuits and fry bacon. Cleaning up the mess, she gazed across the wide river. How clean the water was with gentle currents. There were no big rocks or boulders to get in the way of a successful crossing. All of this worrying is over nothing, she thought, with the men finishing the flatboats to cross peaceful waters.

While Angelina sat next to Jacque eating their quick breakfast of coffee that she had grown to love with sugar, biscuits with orange marmalade, dried apples, and the bacon she fried for her and Jacque. They listened while the men spoke of the two rivers, the Ohio River and Muskingum River that they were to cross to get to Marietta in the Ohio Territory. Marietta was at the mouth of the Muskingum River on the Ohio River, which was where they were informed was their landing spot.

At ten o'clock, the men were ready. They had slept in late to ready themselves for the day. At first, the oxen shook the flatboat. Angelina stood between the two oxen and held their reins while speaking softly to keep them calm. She watched Jacque use the long stick slowly to push off the bottom on the right side of the raft. On the left side, Henri had decided to join their flatboat to help row since he had broken up his wagon to use for more wood to build Angelina's and Jacque's flatboat. Now, they were destined to carry along Henri in their wagon. Henri had announced to the wagon party that after the river crossing, they would be in Marietta by sunset.

Angelina was all jitters. Inside her belly, the butterflies fluttered with anxiety. She was wondering if the flatboat would make it. The only thing that made her feel secure was the fact that she had two manly men helping her. She felt lucky that all she had to do was stand and look around her.

Chapter 19

A ngelina studied the land and river. It had a rugged, untouched beauty that hypnotized her. Green, blooming trees of every kind, the gentle lapping of blue water, and blue-sky overhead that looked like it would never end. She started to relax as she looked down into the water to see if she could spot fish. Angelina had never seen anything like it. She thought the water was so clean and clear. Tired of ignoring the filth on her, tired of smelling the smoke of the campfires, the smell of pork and beans that permeated her clothing. She wanted to bath in it. At times, Angelina felt nauseous when her mind came back to the Native American man that attacked her. She needed to wash the touch of him off her. Once they sailed down the Ohio River, she had never felt so calm and relaxed now that they were out of danger with the anticipation of a Shawnee attack. Later tonight, Angelina thought, she should write of the attack to Thomas Jefferson, and knew she had to draw him a picture of what the Shawnee Native man looked like to show him in her letter.

The majestic river curved at wide angles that flowed the river smoothly, peacefully up to flowing together of the two rivers. She studied the river. Angelina observed animals that she never expected to see; deer with antlers, a big doe with her fawns, geese and ducks dunking their heads down into the water. In spite of getting caught up in her new surroundings, she kept her wits about her to be on the lookout along the river's edges watching for violent Native Americans. She still had the lingering sense that the Shawnee, or any other Native could easily see the wagon party. Meanwhile, to make the time go by faster, the three French friends made small talk.

"I have never questioned you two about how or why you came to cross over her," said Henri, "but do you plan on settling on in Marietta?"

Angelina and Jacque looked at each other in the awkward silence. Should they, or shouldn't they speak of their past, their destination, and who would speak first.

Angelina nodded.

"Henri, "Angelina began, "we are not settling in Marietta. We plan on going to the Island of Mackinac up north further."

"May I ask why?"

"We are going to live with my uncle."

"Really," said Henri with a curious air, "What is he doing up there?"

"He is a fur trapper from what he writes me."

"Why that sounds like a good life to me."

"What are you going to do Jacque? Are you going to be a fur trapper yourself? You look like a capable, strong lad."

"I am going to have my own shoe shop."

"Oh, so you are a man of skills. You will do well for yourself. Everyone needs shoes, and we all have a need for different kinds of shoes."

"Yes, my father made shoes and so will I."

"Good man, I know your father must have taught you well, confident as you are."

After one month and a half of traveling in a wagon, the wagon party arrived in Marietta, Ohio. Henri passed on the news that informed him about traveling up to the Straits of Mackinac, which was where Lake Huron and Lake Michigan met in the middle. He learned that this Mackinac Island was in the middle of the Straits of Mackinac, and he needed to speak to Angelina and Jacque about it.

"From the heads of the settlement, they say that the nearest port to travel up to Mackinac Island is to be at Port Cleveland. You two are going to have to travel in the wagon north up to Lake Erie that looks like an ocean of water, so say the men. Then, at Port Cleveland, you have to sail over the great blue waters on Lake Erie, and onwards north up to Lake Huron and Lake Michigan waters where they meet.

It is named, they say the 'Straits of Mackinac'. There you two would arrive while traveling on a cargo ship in the middle of the Straits is Mackinac Island."

· Jacque left Angelina to trade their tired oxen for new ones. She climbed into the camped wagon getting out her diary to make notes of the inventory of their provisions that they would need to be replacing.

Once she looked into what they had, she noticed that they were down much more flour, sugar, and salt pork than what she had calculated. Could it be that someone had come in their wagon to steal some of their food supplies? She was furious knowing who was to blame. Maybe it wasn't just Helen, she thought, perhaps other people had helped themselves, or maybe she calculated wrong.

As she walked to the Marietta General Store to buy more of what they needed, Angelina observed everything around her to remember it all. She walked past wealthy looking men wearing black tri-corner hats and soldiers that wore bluecoats. Some men Angelina passed wore common breeches. The women wore plain dresses, she thought, these people looked ordinary to her compared to the fashionable attire that she was used to seeing when she had lived at Versailles. These settlers looked like they had hard lives living off the land, yet, comfortable lives compared to the peasants of France who were governed by the royal family. France's royal family had needed the commoners to do everything for them. Feed them, sew their clothes with fancy lacework for them, help dress them daily, and clean up after them.

The Americans had won their revolution, she thought, but still the people looked so poor. She couldn't tell that they had won anything, but another set of responsibilities away from the British king.

Coming back after buying the provisions, Henri walked towards Angelina,

"How do you like it here, Mademoiselle?"

"I am ready to move on as soon as possible." She noticed Henri biting his lip. "Henri, is something bothering you?"

"No, it is just that some of the wagon party is going to settle here. I have bought a wagon from one of the party. They can use the money to build their home with new wood. The rest of the wagon party will separate as they decide where they will settle north. I was wondering, do you mind if I tag along with you and Jacque to this Mackinac Island of yours that you're headed for? I can't get it out of my mind. I would like to see it for myself. I could trap again, if there is a fur company up there that will have me."

"I don't see why not. I would love it if you came with us. I will speak with Jacque. I think that you could find your fortune there since my uncle has made a life for himself up there."

"I will speak to Jacque myself, mademoiselle. Adieu, I have to buy some things before we leave tomorrow. I hear it's going to take up to two weeks to get to Port Cleveland."

Once the wagon party rolled out of Marietta, Ohio on route again, Angelina vowed that she would catch Helen. The young bride and groom rode along in the wagon party to settle down north to where the groom's brother lived in the territory north called Michigania, which was the territory just below where Mackinac Island was.

Angelina's mind raced with scenarios as she struggled with deciding what she would do if she caught Helen inside her wagon. Should she confront her? Should she just let it go, so that she could avoid a confrontation? Maybe the new married couple were poor, maybe her husband made her, or perhaps it was all in her head and Helen was innocent.

In the late afternoon, the wagon party settled for the night wanting to see the sun set in all its glorious colors. Angelina decided to go out for a walk.

"Jacque, "I'm going out for a walk to look around."

"I'm going to set up camp with Henri," he replied. "Be careful there are Natives out here. Do you want the musket?"

"No, but I will take the knife that you cut up the animals with from hunting."

While she walked in a small wooded area not far from camp, Angelina hid the knife in her apron pocket in the front. She loved the fresh air away from the smoke of the cook fires. Angelina could tell the rain was coming. The air had cooled in the pine scented woods, the sky darkened, and the breeze had picked up.

Suddenly, Angelina saw a girl holding a basket with what looked like raspberries. Angelina was terrified as she stopped and stared at her. It was a Native American girl with straight, shiny black hair that hung down in a braid. She was the most beautiful, exotic girl she had ever seen with her bronze-colored skin. She wore what looked like a shockingly short skirt that hung down just past her knees. Her shirt was a plain deerskin poncho blouse, but it seemed so colorful to Angelina because the poncho was decorated with a long strings of beads around the neck.

Angelina wouldn't or couldn't move. Was the Indian girl ready to attack her? She was prepared to defend herself this time. Angelina held up her hand to wave hello at her. The girl's face softened. Angelina heard footsteps behind her. She turned around, and there was a Native American boy in her face. He looked like the Shawnee she killed with the same hair baldness on the sides of his head except for one straight lock of hair that stood straight up the middle from his forehead down to the back, and he had two black feathers that came off the back of his head."

"Don't scream," he said calmly in English.

"Are you going to hurt me?" She looked at him intently as she studied his profile. A hooked nose, high cheekbones, bronze-colored skin, and white teeth. He looked young, tall and lean wearing animal-hide leggings with tassels hanging from them and no shirt. She couldn't take her eyes off his hands that held his bow and arrow.

"No. Why would I?"

Angelina wasn't going to answer that. "You speak English?"

"As you can see."

Angelina blushed from embarrassment.

"Sorry, I didn't mean anything by it. Where did you learn to speak English? I have never spoken to a Native before."

"That doesn't surprise me. My father was an Englishman and mother Wyandot. That is my wife. We were out hunting together."

"But you look like you are old as me and you are married."

"We are seventeen summers. How old are you?"

"Fourteen."

"So are you married?"

"No. I have no beau."

"But you will be soon enough." And he chuckled. "How is it that you are here?"

"I am traveling north to be with my uncle who lives in the Northwest Territory on Mackinac Island. Forgive me for my asking, but you are so young to be married, is this usual for your people?"

"Yes, it is so. Where did you come from?"

"France," answered Angelina. "May I ask what your tribe is called?"

"It is called Wyandot," the Native American boy answered, "but the French settlers call us Huron. 'Hur' means 'head of boars' and 'on' means 'people'."

"Oh, so your hairstyle sets you apart. I have seen a Shawnee man with the same hair, though. How are you different from the Shawnee?"

"They are of a different Nation of people. They are fierce, violent warriors. We are peaceful, farming people."

"I understand," said Angelina politely, feeling as if she ought to leave.

"It's good to know that there are nice Indians in this new country." She was starting to feel the conversation coming to an end. "I have to go now. It was very nice to meet you. Maybe, if you ever go north. You can come visit me on Mackinac Island.

You would be welcome. I have an Ottawa aunt that my uncle has married."

"Thank you," he replied. "Maybe in the summer we could try and go up there."

Angelina felt as if she had walked for hours to clear her head for her feet ached as much as her head did from overthinking. Why did Native Americans get married so young? The only boy she knew was Jacque. She loved Jacque. Could she see herself loving him? Someday becoming his wife? He never gave her the impression either that he cared for her in that way.

Yes, they were close. They were each other's confidant. They had been through a lot together in the small amount of time they had known each other. She had been his only support when Philippe was buried at sea. She liked the thought of him, he was handsome to her. Could he ever love her? Jacque was strong-minded, confident, and had a strong desire to become his own man with his shoe shop. She admired him for his goals.

As Angelina walked back towards her wagon delighted with thoughts of him, she saw movement inside her wagon and excited to see Jacque. She wanted to wait to tell him how she felt about him until they reached Mackinac Island. She wanted to see if he was interested in other women, or should she just tell him? Arriving back at her wagon, she opened the back-wagon. There she was, Helen.

Without any hesitation, Angelina jumped in, grabbed the back Helen's dress, and yanked her out with a gratifying thud! Helen landed on her back. Angelina jumped out and faced her. Everyone rushed over to see what all the uproar was about.

"Did Jacque say you could come into our wagon?"

"I'm sorry. No one was here, so I figured you wouldn't mind pitching in for supper."

"I do mind," she yelled, "never go into my wagon! You don't have permission to go into my wagon!"

Jacque and Henri ran over to them from Henri's wagon eager to see what was going on. Angelina glared at the on-lookers furious.

"And you all can stop looking at Jacque and me as people to be taken advantage of! We are not sharing with anyone anymore! What's ours is ours! Enough is enough of thinking that you can take from us just because there's only the two of us!"

She straightened her mobcap while she looked back at the settlers from the wagon party staring at her. There was an awkward silence that lingered around her with the crowd staring at her after her outburst. Jacque took her hand in his and led her back up to the wagon and closed the flap. They sat down together on the bed across from each other.

"Angelina, you did it. You stood up for yourself. I have never seen you like that. I didn't know if you could ever do it. You stood up for yourself in front of everybody. I am so proud of you. How do you feel?"

"I feel released of all the anger I have felt over being used." She blushed at his compliments.

"Helen will leave you alone now," he chuckled. "We have saved our supplies to get us to Mackinac Island without running short. Be proud of yourself, Angelina. I can tell this is the first time that you have ever stood up for yourself. It will get easier to do now. Now that you have done it once."

"Jacque, won't you always be with me to help me when I am not confident when I am not strong?"

"Angelina, you won't need me. You don't need me now. You can take care of yourself. You have taken care of yourself even before we met in Paris."

"I guess I did, but Jacque," as her heart ached at the thought of him leaving her, "do you plan on leaving me once we get to Mackinac Island."

"I haven't thought of it. Why? Are you asking me to leave?"

"No, I don't want you to leave. I want to make sure you are safe," said Angelina blushing, not wanting to give away her real feelings.

Within two weeks, they arrived in Port Cleveland on the shore of Lake Erie. Anxiety and the excitement of the journey getting to Mackinac Island was almost over that it consumed her thoughts. The three French friends booked passage on a bulk cargo schooner that was headed for Mackinac Island to drop a shipment of goods off for the soldiers at the fort. They were to sail overnight up the vast blue waters of Lake Erie, the Detroit River, Lake St. Clair, St. Clair River, and into Lake Huron. Angelina and Jacque stood on the top deck. She touched his hand on the railing.

"Jacque, I'm glad we're here together."

"I wish Phillipe," Jacque hesitated to speak, "could be here to see this."

"I think Phillipe is looking down on us. He is protecting us. I think our families are looking down on us, happy for us."

And he nodded his affirmation with his head down and eyes closed. Angelina watched him while he tried to shake off his tears of sadness. She slowly, silently walked away, and left him alone to shed his tears for his little brother.

Chapter 20

Afentter two months of traveling by mid-June, the three friends slept through a rainy night. The next morning the lake shimmered in the sunlight. Clear blue skies and light breezes blew across Lake Huron as the schooner anchored into the calm waters of the natural harbor at Mackinac Island.

Angelina's eyes marveled at the little island. It looked like an enchanted island that sprung out of the water. Grey gulls, white-winged heron, and loons lingered around the rocky shoreline. While the schooner approached the dock, Angelina studied the coastline. She was amazed to see masses of Native American men, women and children crowded along the shores of the island. Hundreds of teepees were camped together on the rocky shore.

The Natives all seemed to look the same. The closer she analyzed them, she observed different hairstyles, clothes, and markings on their faces and arms.

Staring at the cliffs, Angelina pointed out to Jacque and Henri, the huge white-washed buildings of Fort Mackinac overlooking the harbor sheltered with what looked like a long and tall white-washed brick wall.

"That is a fort, mademoiselle," said Henri. "We will have to find out who governs that fort. I hope for our fortunes that the Americans control the fort. If it is the British, they can be a nasty lot. Whoever governs that fort, governs this island."

Angelina, Jacque, and Henri left the wooden boxes with their belongings safe with the crew of the schooner until they agreed to pick them up later that day. Their senses overflowed with the smell of horse-manure and smoke from the cook fires from where the Native Americans camped. They tried to get away from the smells by walking immediately onto the main street of the Island's busy town.

"For such a small island," Angelina stated, "it is as busy as Paris was."

Jacque and Henri nodded.

Each in their private thoughts, they were swept up in the sounds, sights, and smells surrounding them.

Angelina looked up at Henri for his usual confident, self-assured manner, but he looked like a lost child. Angelina turned her head to look at Jacque. He appeared to her as if the island didn't intimidate him. He walked with his head held high. His eagle eyes darted everywhere around. She felt her heart flutter with a different kind of butterflies. He had grown taller, grown some hair on his chest hair that poked out of his V-neck white peasant shirt. She could see how muscular his arms had grown bigger underneath his sleeves since they had first met on the streets on Paris.

"We need to find my uncle."

"I agree," Jacque answered, "and then we will know where we will sleep and eat. I'm getting hungry."

"Sounds good," replied Henri, "Uncle Claude will know how I may go about finding myself in the fur game."

While they wandered down the main street, the three looked silently at four soldiers wearing redcoats passing by. Henri took it upon himself to make some conversation."

"Good day, garcons," greeted Henri. "We are in need of some assistance. Could you please advise us where the fur trade post is?"

"Up at Fort Mackinac, of course," said the blond soldier, as he sneered, curling his lip at them. "You just get here from France or Canada?" He asked, turning towards his group of soldier friends and chuckled.

"We have just got off a schooner from Lake Erie," answered Jacque. "Why does it matter to you where we came from?" he asked with his temper flaring and his fists clenched.

Henri stepped in front of Jacque as the soldiers went for their swords.

"Garcons, you will have to excuse my friend for his boldness. Yes, we just got off a schooner. He is just tired and hungry. Don't mind him. Thank you for your assistance again."

The three quickly walked away towards the fort.

"Hey Frenchy's'," the blond soldier shouted after them.

They all turned around, curious to know what would happen next, Angelina turned around sick with her stomach in knots.

"Just to let you know that Americans don't own Fort Mackinac. England does-we do. We control everything that goes on this island."

"Good to know," stated Henri. "However, with the Americans winning the revolution, how do you British still manage to have control of the fort?"

"We have our ways Frenchy. We have our ways."

"Good day to you." Henri tipped his tri-corner hat to the British soldiers. He turned back around and rolled his eyes. He looked at Angelina and Jacque. "Let's move," he whispered where only they could hear.

With the heat of the afternoon sun burning down on their backs, they trudged up the steep hill to the fort.

After asking around among groups of British soldiers, French trappers and fur traders, they found a few of the French trappers who knew Claude Savoy very well. Angelina listened to their stories about him and Mackinac Island. She learned that Fort Mackinac was the largest fur trading center, which was the reason why the British still wanted to control Mackinac Island since it brought an enormous profit to the British. Claude Savoy had not returned to the island yet to trade his winter furs for British goods. Angelina did discover that he shared a house with a few other fellow French trapper friends.

The three friends located his little wood cabin. It was a simple log, one-story house with a very high picket fence that ran all the way up and down the road. The three decided to separate and meet back at the little log cabin later by sunset.

Getting her wooden boxes carried to her cabin, she unpacked the rest of the provisions, the leather bag, and her beloved tapestry bag that was inside wooden boxes.

Once Angelina got settled, she cleaned and dusted the little house. She located the General Store to see what they sold for food and supplies. She made some ham and cheese sandwiches for Jacque, Henri, and a couple of trappers that came back for a meal and a bed. Angelina waited for her uncle who never arrived.

Under the lantern light often on summer nights in the little log cabin, she wrote Mr. Thomas Jefferson a few letters and wrote Kiara too.

She notified him that she had arrived. In one letter, she informed him of her adventures from the last leg of her journey from Marietta, including a drawing of what the Native American married couple looked like.

In the other letter, she wrote her thoughts of Mackinac Island. Finally, she wrote how she was enjoying the summer nights while she drew pictures for Mr. Jefferson using the colored pencils and parchment that he gave her of what the Ohio River looked like and what Mackinac Island looked like.

She also decided to write him about what had happened with Helen. I wonder if Mr. Thomas Jefferson will show this letter to President George Washington, she thought. Mr. Jefferson said he did want to know everything that happened.

She pulled out her uncle's letter and read it again. She reflected over the idea that since he married an Ottawa Indian woman that he would live with her Indian people from now on. Maybe he would never come back, she assumed, perhaps she would never meet him. He didn't know she was here. No one knew where he was, so there was no one to get a message to him.

How long would she have to wait until he returned to this enchanted island? What would she do in the meantime while she waited for him to arrive?

Chapter 21

O ver the summer weeks of waiting, Angelina had purchased with the money from the jewels a few acers of land on the north side of Mackinac Island to build a dairy farm of her own with Jacque and Henri. She also managed to help Jacque build his shoe shop. This was another first for her that she could finally witness Jacque's great skill at making shoes. She loved that she was lucky. She thought that she would always have pretty slippers. Henri had been a great help as her farmhand taking care of the cows that she had purchased. Angelina managed the chickens with their eggs and feeding pigs. Both of her men had been kind enough to kill the pig and chickens when they needed one for dinner, and she would cook and preserve them for winter months how James Hemmings had taught her at Monticello.

Over the water, the sailing ships and canoes from the south mainland brought the news of what was happening in the world. Angelina had discovered from one of her uncle's French trapper friends that the royal family in France were still imprisoned in the Tuileries Palace under surveillance, a limited house arrest under the watchful eyes of the Guard Nationale. A new law changed that overruled Louis XVI. The new law ruled now that the Assembly and the king would share the right to declare war. Angelina worried that this new law would be the first of many, she thought, to destroy the king's power. The Assembly would eventually take all the control over the country, and then what would happen to them. She prayed for Queen Marie for the mother that she had been to her, Princess Marie and little Louis Charles. She would forever remember her past with France's princess with fondness and cherish the memories of the life that they had spent together.

Toward the middle of August, Angelina accepted that Uncle Claude and she would never meet since he thought that she was still in France.

She grew to love the beautiful island as she walked over the entire island a little at a time. Swimming along the rocky shoreline, spending the twilight hours walking the east and west bluffs with Jacque, and staring down on the turquoise waters of the great lakes.

Angelina had spent hours discovering all the nature of the island's woods. The useful maples to tap for syrup next winter. Along with elms, cedars, beech trees that reached up to the sky. She loved the colorful forest floor of wildflowers, the chorus of birdsong that perched on the trees, and the numerous little fresh springs that ran all over the Mackinac Island.

Once a week, Angelina walked to town to pick up supplies and to people watch. She walked past the windows of little shops to see the shoppers. She observed the local Natives Americans on shore, walked into Jacque's shoe shop to chat, and hiked up to Fort Mackinac to ask the other French trappers if they had seen her uncle, hoping for news of him.

One hot August Saturday, after a refreshing swim in the great lakes, she made her rounds to meet Jacque and walk home. She hiked up to the fort first before everyone left for the day. At long last, she learned that her Uncle Claude Savoy had come to the island.

Unexpectedly, she feared meeting him. What if he did not want to meet her? How would she react, if she was right and he didn't want her around because he had a family of his own with his Ottawa wife? She would be devastated after coming all this way to be with him.

She slowly made her way to her small farm pondering how she would meet him. What would she say when they finally met each other? She thought long and hard during her walk home. What she would say and how she would react to meeting him face to face.

During the night hour, he still hadn't come. She decided to write her daily letter to Mr. Thomas Jefferson by oil lamp. Angelina jumped, startled when she heard someone knocking at the front door. Angelina thought it must be Jacque since she had forgotten to meet him because the news of her Uncle Claude had shocked and distracted her.

Opening the door, she was looking at a five-foot-tall, dirty blond hair, heavy-set man with slabs of muscles showing through his V-neck peasant shirt, and buckskin breeches.

"Uncle Claude," she said softly.

"Yes," He reached his arms out to her.

She jumped into his arms. All her fears and doubts faded as she looked at him with tears in his eyes. Angelina's heart felt as if it was in her throat.

"Oh, I am so happy to meet you," Angelina choked out.

"Angelina," Claude Savoy declared, "I can't believe that you are standing in front of me. I often thought of you coming here to the New World and Mackinac Island."

"I am so glad to finally meet you. I have brought with me wine from France for you." Her whole manner said the things Angelina couldn't say. It didn't have to be spoken out load.

In the end, Angelina's words were cut off as she was swung around, hugged, and then gathered into her uncle's strong arms in a little dance.

Angelina needed no one to take care of her. She had a grown up into a courageous, strong, and independent woman. Angelina owned a quaint farm on this enchanted island called Mackinac Island. She welcomed her Uncle Claude Savoy into her home, for they had years worth of conversations to make up for.

Made in the USA
Middletown, DE
26 March 2023

27505490R00118